The Best in Me

Nicole Scott

ISBN:978-1-7363032-8-3

DEDICATION

To Seanita and Scott.
You bring out the best in me.

ACKNOWLEDGMENTS

First giving honor to God for whom all my blessings flow. I am thankful to my parents for all the love and support they have shown me my entire life even when I didn't appreciate it. Mom, I love you more than I can say. Daddy I wish you had the opportunity to read my debut novel. I love and miss you.

My two children are the best things I've ever done. Each of you has given me a reason to keep going when I wanted to quit. I am very proud of you and will continue to expect great things from you.

I belong to a wonderful book club that has been reading books, traveling, and having fun together for over twenty-five years. We’ve seen each other through weddings, babies, divorces, and deaths. Keep reading ladies.

A special thank you to authors Karen E Quinones Miller and Stacy Lawrence for helping me. Kelli, Vernon, Kemba, Ceasar, LaRubia, and Shonda, keep writing.

Part One

One Monkey Don't Stop No Show

1

August 1990

They weren't supposed to open the door. Their mom had given them strict instructions not to answer if anyone ever dropped by unannounced. But April couldn't keep ignoring the disturbance their persistent visitor was making by knocking. April was going to have to get rid of whoever it was. When Junior finally got off the couch, April grabbed his arm to pull him back down. He snatched it away and turned toward his big sister. She raised a finger to her mouth and cut her eyes at him. From prior experiences, he knew better than to open his mouth or move, but that didn't stop him from glaring back at her. Brooklyn was too engrossed in singing along with a Janet Jackson video to pay the knock any attention.

April slipped out of her shoes, tiptoed to the door, and peeked through the peephole. She stepped back and covered her mouth when she saw the woman standing there. They only lived a few minutes away from each other but they hadn't seen her in a long time. The last time she was at their apartment their mom ordered her to leave and told her not to ever come back.

Her grandmother knocked again, harder this time. April released a deep breath, turned the knob, and reluctantly opened the door just enough to stick her head out and talk. But not wide enough to give the impression that she was welcome to come inside.

Taking a small step forward, her grandmother had a huge smile across her face when she said, "Hey baby. Look at you. You're getting so big."

Her hair was much longer than April remembered it. And she had apparently given up on dye and let her gray hair have its way. Other than that, her grandmother looked exactly the same. She was still a pretty dark-skinned full-figured woman with only a few wrinkles. Before April could figure out an excuse to get rid of their unexpected guest, her younger brother and sister bolted towards the door. They recognized the familiar voice in the hallway. Junior pushed her out of the way and yelled, "Move out the way April. We wanna let Grandma in."

Their grandmother eased her way past the gatekeeper and stepped inside. April watched as she reached for Brooklyn and Junior, who were equally enthused about seeing her. "Oh my God. Let me look at y'all. All of you are getting taller. Grandma missed you so much."

"We missed you too, Grandma," they said simultaneously.

As they held onto each other tightly, April noticed Grandma's nose wrinkle like she smelled something horrible. She watched as her grandmother looked over the kids' shoulders at the two large black trash bags overflowing in the corner of the kitchen. Then at the sink which was full of caked-on dishes. As if on cue, a gigantic roach crawled across the kitchen countertop. April bit her bottom lip and wished they had cleaned up.

She stood helplessly as Grandma released her grip on them and examined Brooklyn's hair. With her braids loose, it was practically standing up on top of her head now. April wanted to tell her that she had just taken the braids out to comb it when Brooklyn jumped up because Janet Jackson was on, but she probably wouldn't believe her. Then she grabbed Junior's chin and moved his head from left to right to get a good look at his lint-filled afro. April knew that his hair hadn't been cut in months. And he gave off a tart smell because she hadn't made him take his bath yet.

Their grandmother folded her arms across her chest and frowned. Her eyes swept April's body up and down like she was inspecting her as well. April quickly put her head down to avoid direct eye contact. But her grandmother moved closer and touched her chin and lifted up her head. They stared at each other for a few seconds. April could see the tears welling up in her grandmother's eyes. She closed them for a second to massage her forehead. Then the silence ended and Grandma bombarded April with a million questions. "Who's been cooking y'all dinner?"

"Me," April answered and folded her arms across her chest.

"Have y'all been going to school every day?"

"Yes."

"When was the last time your hair was combed?"

April shrugged.

"Why didn't you call me?"

This time April rolled her eyes but didn't respond.

She took care of her younger siblings as well as she could. Her mother never taught her how to cook. So Ramen noodles, peanut butter and jelly sandwiches, hot dogs, and cereal were the best she could do.

April made sure that her siblings went to school. But sometimes she skipped school to be with her boyfriend. Her little sister was tender-headed and wouldn't sit still long enough for her to do a halfway decent job on her hair unless she popped her on her leg with the plastic comb. Then her brother would get mad at her and they'd all be ready to fight. And how was she supposed to call anyone when their phone had been disconnected for the last few months?

Her grandmother was an adult, not her. She should have known what her daughter was doing. Everyone else did.

April watched her take a deep breath and grabbed the small gold cross that hung from her necklace. This meant that she was trying to calm down. Her grandmother looked into the faces of the younger two. But they were looking at April waiting to see what their big sister was going to say. "It's okay. Grandma is here now." When they turned their attention back to her she continued, "I want all of you to go grab your toothbrushes and some clothes. Y'all are going to stay at my house for a little while."

"For real? "Brooklyn shrieked.

"Yes," Grandma said, matching her grandbaby's excitement. "Now go get your things."

Brooklyn and Junior looked at each other and then ran towards their rooms celebrating before April could stop them. She threw her hands up in the air, turned to her grandmother, and yelled, “Why did you do that? Mama is gonna be mad when she gets back and we’re not here. We can’t go with you.”

“Baby, you don’t understand. Your mother is the one who sent me over here to get you.”

“Mama called you?” April’s mouth twisted to the side. None of this made any sense. She used to spend so many nights crying herself to sleep because she didn’t know where her mother was. Now that she was used to being home alone with her siblings, her grandmother shows up out of the blue telling them what to do. Who did she think she was? They hadn’t seen her in two years. Why was she so interested in them now? With no attempt to hide her flippant tone or to make this exchange easy, April questioned, “Why would Mama call you?”

“I’ll explain what’s going on when we get to my house. Go pack so we can leave.” April didn’t move an inch. Her grandmother’s expression made it clear she didn’t appreciate it. So did her voice, which was much sterner this time. “Now, April.”

April raised an eyebrow and stared the woman in front of her down. She knew that she was being disrespectful to her elder. But her grandmother was going to have to tell her something if she wanted her to move.

Her grandmother exhaled and announced, “Your mother is in jail April.

2

Mary's heart sank every time she stepped into the lobby to visit her only child in Fulton County Jail. But despite how troubled Felicia sounded over the phone, when she appeared in the visiting room, she actually looked better than she did at their first visit a few weeks ago. Mary had to suppress her smile. Felicia's hair was neatly parted down the middle with two thick braids on both sides. Even though she was still skinnier than her normal weight, Felicia's face appeared to be fuller like she had gained a few pounds in here. As much as she complained about how nasty the food the jail served was, that let Mary know that she wasn't eating at all before she was forced to stop running the street and sit still.

Felicia plopped down in her seat and immediately started complaining. "Mama you've got to get me out of here. Some of these women are crazy. At night, my cellmate keeps me awake talking about what the voices in her head are telling her to do," Felicia whispered into the phone.

Mary closed her eyes and shook her head imagining Felicia being locked up with an insane woman. She wondered if the guards allowed her to take medicine.

Her daughter twirled her braid around her finger when she asked, "How much do you think your house is worth? You can use it as collateral to get me out of here."

Mary rubbed her hands up and down her thigh and exhaled. "Baby, are you really asking me to put up my house? You know if you miss one, just one, court date they'll take it away from me."

Felicia tried to plead with her mother. "Mama, you know I'd never do that to you."

"I didn't know that you were a crackhead. How would I know what you would do?" The words flew out of Mary's mouth before she realized what she was saying.

Felicia sat up straight. Mary noticed her eyes shot left and then right, surveying the visiting room to see if anyone on her mother's side had overheard. Mary covered her mouth. She looked at the person on the next phone. The lady's eyes met hers before she averted her gaze and turned her attention back to the woman she was visiting. Embarrassed, Mary wanted to light into Felicia for her careless actions, but this probably wasn't the time or the place.

After a few moments of uncomfortable silence, Mary spoke up. She was there to put a little money on Felicia's account and let her know that her kids were being well taken care of now that she had them. But so far her daughter didn't seem concerned about her offspring. "Aren't you going to ask about your kids?"

"Sorry. Got a lot on my mind." Felicia continued to twirl her new braid. "Are the kids getting on your nerves?"

"The other night after Junior's nightly shower, I noticed that the bar of soap in the tub was dry as a bone and his towel wasn't even damp. But the next night I was ready for him. I barged into the bathroom after the shower had been running for a few minutes. The hot water had the room full of steam and I caught him fully dressed sitting on the bathroom floor playing with his handheld game wasting all my hot water. I tore his behind up with my belt." Mary felt triumphant when she stated, "I bet he won't try that again."

Felicia covered her mouth and her eyes grew larger. Mary folded her arms across her chest. She didn't understand what was so funny. After she finally caught her breath and finished giggling, Felicia said, "I'm sorry Mama. I know you aren't used to raising boys. But boys are nasty. That's what they do. You have to really watch them. I'm sure he will just learn to be better at it next time."

Mary shook her head and continued. "Brooklyn is fine. That child talks nonstop, but I've learned how to tune her out if I have to. I wouldn't be surprised if she grew up to be a reporter." Mary waved her hand in front of her face like she was swatting a gnat. "You already know the trouble I've been having with April, but I can't afford to raise my blood pressure any more than it already is right now."

Felicia shook her head that she understood. She used the break in the conversation to begin talking about herself again. "I went to court today and I've got a horrible public defender. If I stick with him, I know I'm goin' to jail for a long time Mama." She paused for a moment.

Mary braced herself for what was coming next.

"Do you think that you could at least use some of your savings to get me a new lawyer? A better lawyer could get my charges lowered or get me a decent plea bargain. I would serve less time and I'd be back to get my kids off your hands a lot sooner." Her eyes were pleading as much as her mouth was. "I promise I'm gonna do right this time Mama."

A guard's voice interrupted the hushed whispers in the room. "Visiting time is over."

Mary was relieved she didn't have to have to continue this discussion. "I'll see what I can do Felicia." She quickly stood up to leave, "You stay out of trouble. You hear?" She placed the phone back on the receiver not caring if her daughter answered her or not.

As she walked back to her car, Mary thought about what her desperate child had asked her to do. She told herself that there was no way that she would put her house up for collateral. But she knew she didn't have enough money saved to bond Felicia out of jail without help. At fifty-two, she was still trying to get her finances together. When she was married if she didn't get to her husband before he started drinking, he would drink up the bulk of his paycheck leaving her to foot most of the household bills alone. Her warehouse check was small, so she had to stretch it as far as she could. Despite his foolish behavior over the years, they were finally able to pay off the house right before he passed. Once he died, his life insurance check allowed her to fix up her house and semi-retire for a while to grieve. Her bubbly personality helped her to make ends meet by selling

Avon, swearing never to stand up all day at work again. But now that she had three extra mouths to feed, she may have to get another job.

Her daughter's comment about getting her kids off her hands didn't go unnoticed. Felicia thought that she would jump at the chance to get rid of the kids. But Mary knew that being with their drug-addicted mother wasn't what was best for them. She couldn't believe that her child was part of this crack epidemic the country was experiencing. Felicia would have to stay where she was for now.

As she thought about keeping the kids she realized what a change it was for her life. It had been a long day. She got up early to get her three grandkids fed and off to two different schools. Then she volunteered at Mt. Zion for a few hours before she had to endure being patted down at the jail. But her day wasn't over, she moved through the grocery store as quickly as her legs would let her, hurrying back to meet her grandkids when they got home from school. Groceries had to be put away, dinner had to be cooked, homework had to be checked, bath water had to be drawn, and hair had to be braided before she could get some rest and turn around and do the same thing tomorrow.

As she tended to Brooklyn's head, the chatter began. "Grandma, Mercedes had on the cutest dress today. It was purple with rhinestones all across the front of it. I wish I had a dress like that." There was a quick pause. "Did I tell you that Demarco was the only one who couldn't get chocolate milk today? He got smart with our teacher so he had to drink regular white milk. And even though he had a dollar, she wouldn't let him buy an ice cream sandwich. He was so mad, Grandma. We thought he was gonna cry. But that's what he gets for being bad, right?"

A distracted, "I guess so," was all Mary could manage before her grandbaby started gossiping again.

Mary loved all three of them, but some nights their bedtime couldn't come fast enough. Tonight was one of those nights. It was bad enough that she had spent her afternoon listening to her daughter tell her how terrible it was in jail. But then she had to spend her evening with an ungrateful teenage girl, who whined and complained more than the two little ones combined ever could. April was her first born grandchild so they used to have a special bond. It tore Mary up inside that she was now acting so hateful towards her for no reason. The constant attitude, huffing and puffing, rolling of the eyes, one-word answers, and popping of the lips from April had really frayed her nerves.

Mary understood that this whole mess was hard on her. April couldn't seem to understand that everything that was going on was difficult for her too. Mary wasn't going to blow her second chance to be in her grandkids' lives though. But in one day, she'd gone from a quiet house to a noisy house. She was now an instant chauffeur, maid, and cook. She went from coming and going as she pleased, to having to care for three people whose lives depended on her, whether April wanted to admit it or not.

With the children finally asleep, Mary went to her room to read a little before bed. As soon as she turned on her light, the phone rang. For years when her telephone rang, she always knew that it was for her. Now, when it rings, some gum popping little girl or some rusty behind boy was asking to speak to April. So she snatched the phone off the hook.

"Hello."

"Good evening Mary. I'm sorry to call you so late. I just got home and wanted to check on you. I know you had a visit with Felicia today."

The corners of her mouth turned up into a full-fledged smile. Her pastor was so considerate. She needed thoughtfulness today. "Pastor, excuse my tone. I thought you were one of April's little friends calling here again."

"That's alright. Are you okay?"

"I'm fine. Thanks for calling to check on me." She felt like a schoolgirl and sounded like one when her voice got pitchy and high like it was now. "You know, you could've waited until you saw me at church tomorrow to ask me." Not only was he her pastor, but Mary considered Zachariah her friend. Lately, she sensed something special when she was with him at church. But he was taking his sweet time acting on it. She was eager to hear what Zachariah had to say tonight.

"Yes, I know. But I also know that having a loved one in jail is a hard situation to deal with. I wanted to make sure that you know I am always here for you if you need someone to talk to."

Mary took in a big breath and let it out slowly. She wasn't one hundred percent satisfied with his response. Her pastor was a gentleman. But sometimes, she wished that he wasn't. Someone was going to have to make the first move if there was ever going to be anything between them. Call it old-fashioned, but she believed it was the man's job to do the pursuing. But she took her mind off her own needs and thought back to her child.

"Well, to tell you the truth, sometimes I feel like all

of this is my fault. If I hadn't been so judgmental of Felicia, maybe she wouldn't be where she is now. I never forgave her for getting pregnant in high school and throwing her life away."

"No one can fault you for being upset about your baby girl getting pregnant so young. Being a young mother yourself, you knew how hard it was going to be for her."

Mary pulled the covers back and sat down on her bed to try and relax. "I know. But when that no-good drug dealing man of hers ran off leaving her with three kids, I should have been more sympathetic." Mary shook her head. "I didn't like him and thought that she would be better off without him. But I should have shut my mouth and just given her my shoulder to cry on."

Zachariah slowly said, "Mary, you know that you can't blame yourself. Felicia might be your only baby, but she is still a grown woman. You and your husband did a good job raising her." She felt his empathy in his tone. He wasn't judging her or her daughter.

Mary was quiet. She wanted to tell him the truth. That she practically had a shotgun wedding because she was pregnant. Her husband was a horrible provider and spent most of his time at the bar down the street. She was the one at home alone raising Felicia. Mary felt guilty about not telling Zachariah the truth, but not as bad as she would feel about throwing her dead husband under the bus. All she could do was sigh and continued to beat up on herself. "But since her dad died, I spent so much time at church helping with other people's problems, that I couldn't see what Felicia was going through?"

"Mary, did you forget the number of times you went

over to her apartment and knocked on the door? No one can say that you didn't try to stay in her life."

"But I should have tried harder. If not for her, then for my grandbabies." Mary had to get a tissue to wipe the tears that were filling her eyes.

"Felicia knew what that man was selling out there in the streets. She didn't have to stay with him. And she didn't have to start doing drugs either." Zachariah was no longer speaking in a slow concerned tone. Mary could tell Zachariah was trying to snap her out of her self-pity. "She could have called you for help or came to the church that she grew up in. Instead, she pushed everyone away because she knew she wasn't living right. Then when her father died, she only came around with her hand out demanding money, because she thought you had some big insurance check and she should be entitled to half of it."

Mary still wanted to protect her daughter from ridicule. "Pastor, she loved her daddy. I should have known something was wrong with her then when she was acting a fool like that."

"Mary, families act a fool all the time when people die. Maybe it's part of the grieving process to take it out on the people who are left here. I don't know. All I know is you can't beat yourself up about the way other people choose to live their life, even if you were the one that raised them. Let's just pray that she starts to make better choices from here on out."

There was a pause in the conversation for a few seconds. "I guess you're right. She didn't even ask about her kids today until I made her. Who knows what she would do if she got out. As much as I hate to admit it, sitting in jail may do her some good."

3

As soon as April stepped on the porch, the front door swung open. "Where have you been?"

April sighed. *Here she goes again. I haven't even made it inside the house yet.*

"Y'all live with me now and I told you to bring your behind straight home from school."

April stood in the doorway of her grandmother's home, glaring at her short chubby grandmother's pointed finger that was only inches from her face. She carefully maneuvered around her, plopped down on the soft tan couch, and rolled her eyes. April tried to enjoy the cool air from the ceiling fan after being out in the heat, but her grandmother kept fussing.

"Don't you roll your eyes at me, little girl. You may have run wild when you were with your mama, but that ain't gonna happen here."

"Grandma, why are you trippin'? All I did was walk to the mall with my girls." April hoped her rehearsed lie sounded convincing.

Her grandmother removed her hands from her hips as she moved closer to April. "Well, don't your friends have to go straight home from school?"

"No." April raised her eyebrow and took a dig at her grandmother. "Their moms are cool."

Without missing a beat Grandma replied, "I guess that makes me uncool because you have to come straight home. And that's that."

It was obvious that she wasn't going to get any peace in here. Her grandmother was still yelling when April stomped off to the bathroom and slammed the door behind her. She didn't even have to use it, but the bathroom was the only place that she could have any privacy. Her nosey little sister shared a bedroom with her. Her stupid brother was always watching TV in the living room and her grandmother stayed in the kitchen cooking and reading her Bible. This was her only safe haven.

April exhaled and stared at herself in the bathroom mirror. Her hand moved up to her hair as she tried to pull a few strands down to make herself have bangs. Some of the girls at her middle school had hair like the women on TV and in magazines. But she had to suffer a press and curl from her grandmother. She looked like an old lady.

Before her mother went to jail, April never wasted her breath asking to be taken to a salon to get her hair done. She remembered a time when all of them had standing appointments every two weeks. But after her daddy left her mom started crying broke and never stopped. *That whore had money for crack though.*

She wondered if her grandmother would give her the money to get her hair done. April told herself that she would ask her when she wasn't mad at her. But the way things were going, who knew when that would be.

April raised her hands to her cheeks and pinched. She needed some color. With her pale complexion, it was easy to notice the pimples on her face. She shook her head because she was disappointed with what she saw. The girls at school were right when they said she looked plain without eyeliner and lipstick. Every day before she got home she wiped off the makeup that she snuck and put on as soon as she arrived at school each day. A lot of the girls at school wore makeup freely. They didn't have to sneak like she did. Next year, she will be in high school. So she didn't understand why her grandmother was treating her like she was still a little girl.

April turned to the side and looked at her profile in the mirror. "Someone needs to tell that lady that boys had been drooling over my 38 D chest for the last three years. I'm not some little girl."

Since she wasn't ready to face her grandmother again, April decided that she may as well take her bubble bath now. She ran the hot water and sang every word of Mariah Carey's Vision of Love, to try and cool down while she waited for the tub to fill up. April could hear her grandmother clanging pots and pans in the kitchen so she sang louder and spun around as much as the tiny bathroom would permit her to do as she tried to hit the impossibly high notes. About thirty minutes later, as soon as she stepped out of the bathroom wrapped in a towel, her curious younger brother and sister ran up to her. In unison, they asked, "Where were you?"

She popped her lips and said, "Dang, you too? I just went to the mall."

They heard her grandmother yell from the kitchen, "Girl, you'd better watch your mouth. Junior and Brooklyn were just worried about you. You know that they are used to you watching them after school every day."

April plowed through her twelve and ten your old siblings like a bowling ball into pins as she walked to the kitchen to address her grandmother. "Yeah, but that was at home. Mama wasn't around. You're here and Junior is old enough to watch Brooklyn by himself now."

"That's not the only reason you need to come straight home. What about your homework? And don't fix your mouth to lie to me and say that you don't have any either. Your brother and sister already did their homework and their chores." Her grandmother slowly got up from the table and said, "Besides, I cooked us a good dinner and it's getting cold. So hurry up and get dressed so we can eat."

April inhaled and for the first time she got a whiff of dinner. It smelled like country ham, which was one of her favorites, collard greens, and maybe macaroni and cheese. She had to give it to her grandmother; although she got on her nerves with her stupid rules, she was the best cook that she knew. So she ran to put some clothes on. Somehow Grandma's dinner usual meant an end to whatever disagreement that was going on in the house. Cooking for them put her grandma in a better mood. Since April loved her cooking from the time she was a little girl, it was hard to be mad while she was eating it.

After dinner, as she glided the soapy dishrag across the dinner plates, April daydreamed about Brandon who she felt was the only good thing she had going on in her life right now. That's why she risked getting in trouble to hang out with him today after school. She was grateful that her grandma didn't see a glimpse of the fresh hickey on her neck. Her grandmother's strict rule of coming straight home from school every day was going to make her lose him and she couldn't let that happen. When the dishes were finished, she absentmindedly pushed the pile of dirt from one side of the kitchen floor to the other as she hummed her favorite song to drown out her siblings laughing at the TV.

"When you finish in there April," her grandmother called out from the bathroom, "sit down and do your homework."

She mimicked, "When you finish in there, April, sit down and do your homework," in her best old lady voice.

Her grandmother yelled, "What did you say, sweetie? I can hardly hear you."

April burst out laughing because she didn't realize that she was so loud. "Nothing, Grandma."

She looked around at her grandmother's kitchen when she was finished cleaning it. There wasn't a speck of dirt on the countertops or wooden table that she wiped down. Several Tupperware bowls containing leftovers from their dinner were stacked neatly on the sparkling white stove. The kitchen was immaculate now, just the way her grandmother liked it.

Sighing, she sat down to tackle her homework. After about ten minutes of trying to read a story in her Language Arts workbook, April gave up and closed the raggedy old book. She was so distracted trying to figure out how to spend time with her boyfriend that she was still on the same page. Last year, she overdid it and missed so much school hanging out with Brandon that she failed the eighth grade. Most people assumed she was retained because she was dumb, but she made all A's and B's in kindergarten through seventh grade. April learned her lesson. It was very embarrassing for her to be in the eighth grade for the second time when most of her friends were now in high school. But her grandmother paid more attention to her than her mother did. So if she was at school every day and ordered her to come straight home every day, how was she ever going to spend time with him?

Anthony was a sixth grader down the hall at her middle school now. He was getting in trouble in school too. Her younger sister went to an elementary school a few blocks away. She was a different story though. Now a fourth grader, she had been in the Gifted Program since kindergarten because school was her favorite place to be.

April remembered the day she overheard a group of evil women in their apartment building gossiping. "That little one is too smart to be from the same sperm as those other two. You know what they say, Mama's baby. Papa's maybe." All of the ladies laughed together.

Another one added her two cents, "You're right. That youngest one ain't his child. She's too cute and smart. With a mother like that, she could be anybody's baby. Bless her heart."

That night, April went to bed cursing the lying busy-body ladies. She didn't want to believe that they were talking about them, but they were the only family in the building with three kids. So they had to be talking about them. The next day, she woke up looking at her mother differently. She couldn't help thinking that what they said just might be true. Brooklyn was smarter and several shades darker than everyone else. April tried not to, but she never felt the same about her mother after that.

"Did daddy find out? Is that what all the late-night arguing was about? Is that why he never married you, because deep down he knew he couldn't trust you?" These were questions she was never brave enough to ask her mother, but they ran through her mind every time she looked at her. Finally, she convinced herself that the women had to be right.

But April wasn't just frustrated with her mother. In the past three weeks since her grandmother found them in the apartment alone, she was trying to totally change April's life. She was dragging them back and forth to church all the time, and not just on Sundays. They went to Bible study on Wednesday nights and to praise and worship service on Friday nights. They were made to sit still and be quiet for what seemed like forever when she would much rather watch TV or talk on the phone. And if she wasn't making April do more chores than anyone else, she was hounding her about homework. She even seemed irritated when April did everything she was supposed to and got on the phone with one of her friends.

What April really wanted was to be a regular teenager with a boyfriend and a normal family like she used to have. Her mother and father would take care of them and she would never have to worry that either parent wasn't coming back home. Small talk would be made at the dinner table and then everyone would break away and do their own thing for the rest of the night. But it didn't look like she was ever going to have a normal family again. So the least her grandmother could do was to let her have a boyfriend.

Later on, after only getting to watch a couple of TV sitcoms, her grandmother reminded April that it was time for her to go to bed by tapping on her watch. When April didn't react, she gently said, "It's time for you to go to bed, April."

She wasn't impressed with the nice tone of her voice. April was still mad about being scolded for coming home late. Her younger brother and sister had just gone to bed thirty minutes ago. So she decided to take a stand tonight. She stated, "Grandma I don't understand why I have to go to bed so early. I'm five years older than Brooklyn and three years older than Anthony Jr. So why do I only get to stay up thirty minutes later than them? My friends don't have to go to bed this early. I wanna stay up later too."

With a grin on her face, her grandmother quickly replied, "And people in hell want ice water. Now carry your butt to bed."

April stomped away gritting her teeth and mumbling under her breath. "I can't stand living here."

4

It was almost time for Felicia to make the dreaded call to her mother's house. It was the same routine for the month that she'd been locked up. She would try to persuade her mother to bail her out by telling her how horrible it was and her mom would always lie and say she didn't have the money. Then she would hurry up and put one of the kids on the phone so she could get off. Luckily, her mother instructed her not to use up the money on her account by calling more than a couple of times a week.

The guards opened their cell doors after lockdown for dinner time. After she stood in line to get her tray off the cart, Felicia sat at her usual table in their pod. "You want your salad?" Felicia just grinned because they did the same routine all the time. She pushed the salad from her tray to N. O's tray without bothering to answer. In return, her friend pushed the apple sauce onto her plastic tray. It was better not to ask too many questions in jail, so Felicia could only assume her friend's nickname stood for New Orleans. It made perfect sense to her. After all, she named her baby girl Brooklyn because that's where the man she suspected was her daughter's real father was from. When Anthony Sr. asked why she wanted to name her that, she lied and said she just thought it was a unique name.

Ever since she was born, Felicia tried to show Brooklyn special attention. She squeezed her a little tighter for a couple of seconds longer than her other two kids. She always tried to be next to Brooklyn and hold her hand when they went out as a family. The overwhelming guilt that her youngest may have a different father ate away at Felicia's heart all the time. It wasn't Brooklyn's fault that she felt neglected because Anthony Sr. was always in the streets dealing. He was like most men who thought that as long as he paid the bills, that was all he needed to do to keep his woman happy. But Felicia was still a young and attractive woman. If he took her for granted and didn't want to show her any attention, there were plenty of men who did. So one night she gave in to an admirer's flirtation and she messed around without thinking about what she could be jeopardizing.

Telling anyone what she'd done was out of the question. So she dealt with it the best way she could and was determined to take that secret with her to her grave. Whenever April or Junior whined that she favored her, Felicia would simply lie. "I treated both of you the same way when you were little. You just don't remember." They finally stopped complaining and just accepted it as normal.

Felicia was happy that Brooklyn had her grandmother to latch on to now. But that didn't stop her baby girl from whining. "Mommy, when are you coming home?" No matter how many times the family tried to explain the situation to her, she could hear Brooklyn boohooing whenever she called.

Once the ladies finished eating, the mad rush to the four phones on the wall began. Felicia hated waiting to use the phone only to feel worse when she got off. Her mother never agreed to get her out. But she couldn't stop begging because she needed to be free. Not one single hour went by without her wishing she could get high. She started smoking crack to stop thinking about Tony leaving her. Constant thoughts of her first love abandoning her were soon replaced by a constant need to stay high.

Tony's disappearance caused Junior to withdraw into his shell like a turtle. The only thing that seemed to make him happy was playing video games. Since she didn't know how to teach a boy to become a man anyway, Felicia let him deal with missing his dad like that. She reasoned that his head was so busy scoring points or saving kingdoms he wouldn't have time to miss her either, which was a good thing in her mind. But wasting time playing with electronics didn't sit well with his grandmother, who couldn't understand why a kid would rather stay cooped up in the house instead of playing outside like kids did when she was little. Felicia wished her mother would just cut him some slack.

But the main reason she hated calling her family was because of April. She seemed to be handling her dad leaving and her being in jail the worst. It seemed like every time Felicia called, April was in trouble. She had more fights under her belt the last couple of years than the heavyweight champion Mike Tyson did, and there wasn't anything Felicia could do to help sitting in a jail cell.

April had the nastiest attitude in the world towards her. Even though she spent most of her time and energy getting high, Felicia didn't remember her child talking to her with such a smart mouth before she went to jail. Felicia knew that she hadn't always been a candidate for mother of the year. But she was doing the best that she could. It wasn't easy giving up your whole life for a man who walked out on you and never looked back. He took a piece of her heart with him.

She just needed some time to get herself together and figure out what to do with the rest of her life now that Tony was gone. If she could get out of jail, that is. Her mother got on her nerves with her holier than thou attitude. She was always talking down to her about the decisions that she made with her life. One day Felicia just couldn't take it anymore. She snapped at her mom and threw her out of her apartment. When her mother's name showed up on the caller ID, they didn't answer it. And she wouldn't let the kids open the door when she showed up at the apartment no matter how many times she came by. Eventually, her mother gave up.

Two years later, Felicia didn't have a choice but to call her mother to pick up her kids when she got arrested. She was the only person that she had left who she trusted with her kids. But Felicia felt like her mother could help her get out of jail if she wanted to. Her mother probably still had some life insurance money left from when her dad passed away. She was just keeping her locked up out of spite. She kept the kids from her mother, now her mother was keeping the kids from her. Even the Bible says an eye for an eye and a tooth for a tooth.

When she first got arrested, Felicia was sure her mother would give in and bail her out once the kids started getting on her nerves. But maybe her mother liked taking care of them. Maybe her kids would be better off raised by her mother. Her life was in such shambles that she barely knew how to begin fixing it. This possession charge was her first offense. So she hoped that this would all be over soon. But the longer she stayed in jail the more horror stories she heard about the government's war on drugs. How black people were getting serious prison time for crack offenses even if it was the first time they'd ever been in trouble.

Right when it was her turn to use the phone, a woman on one of the other phones talking started looking around and cursing. One woman yelled, "Yo. Why did y'all cut off the phones?" Felicia had a feeling what was coming next. Their cell doors closed halfway indicating that it was time for an emergency lockdown.

All around her women were moaning and complaining. "Somebody did something stupid and now we all gotta get locked down again."

"But we just got let out a few minutes ago," someone else complained.

Two women made a mad dash to the sink with the hot water to pour over their noodles to have something to eat in their cell. No one knew what was going on or if they would be locked in for the rest of the night. Around there, if anyone on any of the floors fought or got into any trouble, the entire jail got locked down as punishment.

Felicia slowly made her way to her cell. She was grateful that she still had a bag of chips and a word search puzzle book that N.O. had loaned her to pass the time. There wasn't much to do in there except watch TV, hoard snacks to eat, talk on the phone, or play Spades. Which meant she was gaining weight and she and her partner N.O. were the reigning Spades champions. Felicia really didn't want to be stuck talking to her bunkmate about the voices in her head for the rest of the night. An officer came in, shut off the TV, which caused more of an uproar with the ladies, and slowly closed all of the cell doors. Felicia rolled her eyes because she knew that she wouldn't get the chance to call her mom or talk to her kids tonight.

5

"Forget you and your fat mama!" April's voice boomed, interrupting Mrs. Johnson's classroom at Sojourner Truth Middle School once again. A male student was struggling to restrain her. But it was proving to be difficult because April was stronger and towered over him. "Let me go. Get off me."

Before anybody knew it, Tiffany, the quietest student in the room, was out of her seat approaching April with a look in her eyes that said that she wasn't backing down today. "I'm sick of you. Say something else about my mama. I know you're not talking about anybody's mama anyway. Everybody knows your mama is a crackhead!"

It was like someone had instructed the entire class to take a deep breath and hold it. They looked around at each other in shock, but no one said a word. A few of them covered their mouths to keep from laughing out loud and becoming April's next target.

Deep down, Mrs. Johnson wished she could just stand there and let them fight. She was one hundred percent certain that Tiffany would release all of her pent-up frustration from being bullied by April and surprise her peers by beating April senselessly. Bringing April down a couple of notches would solve everybody's problem and allow her to get some teaching done. That girl frazzled even her usual calm demeanor. Despite her immense desire to see the underdog win today, her training as a teacher kicked in. "That's enough. Everybody line up. Except for you, April."

After a few giggles and mumbling, the students formed a single file line as instructed. The bell rang and Mrs. Johnson dismissed them from her classroom. As Tiffany walked past, she patted her back and whispered, "Take a deep breath and calm down. It's going to be alright baby." Then she closed the door, walked back to her large wooden desk in the front of the room, and sat down. She took in April's appearance. The cheap red lipstick was too bright for her butterscotch complexion. She stood there glaring back at her with arms folded across her fully developed fifteen-year-old chest. Mrs. Johnson could see the slight movement of her jaw like she was grinding her teeth.

The sound of teenagers yelling and laughing in the hallway had the teen's attention. Turning her head to look at the space under the door, she watched the shadows of the student's feet passing by. Mrs. Johnson knew that she wanted to be out there too.

April let out a heavy sigh. So Mrs. Johnson broke the silence by asking, "Do you know why I'm not letting you leave with the rest of the class?"

April quickly shrugged her shoulder as she stared at the shabby gray carpet in the room. "I guess you wanted to separate Tiffany and me."

Mrs. Johnson let out a heavy sigh of her own. "That was one of the reasons. The other is that because of your constant outbursts and the disrespect to me and your classmates on a daily basis, I'm going to have to call your mother."

The corners of the April's mouth slowly turned up. She closed her eyes and she shook her head from side to side. Then she broke out in a loud laugh like she was sitting in a comedy club and the headliner just told a hilarious joke. Mrs. Johnson wondered what was so funny. April stopped laughing at her confused teacher long enough to say, "My mama's locked up. So I don't think she can come to the phone right now."

Mrs. Johnson, blindsided by the news, ran her hand across her forehead. "I'm sorry. I didn't know that." She stood back up, walked toward April, and tried to touch her arm, but she moved out of her teacher's reach. So she settled for standing with her fingers laced together. After a few seconds of silence, she asked, "So who do you live with then?"

"My grandmother."

She wanted to assure her student that this didn't have to define her life. "April, you aren't the only one with issues. Lots of kids in this school live with their grandparents because their parents are in jail or dead. We have a few kids here who live in foster homes. One of my students even lives in a homeless shelter. Did you know that?"

"No. What's that got to do with me?" she snapped as she rolled her eyes and readjusted her feet to put her weight on her other hip.

Mrs. Johnson sighed. She should have known better than to think she could get this girl to put things in perspective. Kids this age seldom could. "My point is. That's no excuse to behave the way you do."

"Didn't you hear her call my Mama a crackhead?" April spat out. "You just gonna let her get away with that?"

Mrs. Johnson walked away and sat back down in her squeaky chair. She didn't want to seem confrontational to her student. "You started talking about her mother first. Remember? Besides, Tiffany has been turning the other cheek and ignoring your bullying since school started in August. It's October, April. I guess she finally had enough today. And frankly, so have I," she said as she leaned back folded her arms.

April paused for a second and unfolded her arms. She moved closer and stared her dead in her face. "I'm not threatening you, 'cause I know that I would get in trouble if I did. But my grandmother is old. So if you call her getting her all upset -," April didn't finish the sentence. She left it to her teacher's imagination.

Mrs. Johnson's left eyebrow rose and her mouth dropped open. That did it. April had lost her mind. Even with her high heels on, she was much shorter than April. But did that make April think that she could take her on? Was this child really threatening an adult?

The second bell announcing the beginning of the next period rang loudly interrupting their staring contest. April blatantly rolled her eyes, moved to the door, and boldly announced over her shoulder, "I'm going to P.E."

Mrs. Johnson stood up and yelled, "Oh no you're not young lady. Come back here." April's answer to her was a slammed door in her face. She cursed as she grabbed the doorknob. Then she made herself pause and take a few deep breaths before she pulled the heavy wooden door open towards her and stepped out. By this time, April was long gone down the hall. Mrs. Johnson was tempted to march down that same hallway, down the stairs to the gym, and drag the teenager out by her hair. But she wanted to keep her job, so she resisted that urge. Instead, the defeated teacher stomped back into her classroom and slammed the door behind her.

She had sent April to assistant principal Mr. Brown's office a couple times this year for punishment. All the administrator seemed to do was keep April busy for a little while by filing a bunch of papers for him and sending her back to class with a warning. In fact, he'd chastised her and said she should manage her classroom better and stop using him for backup. So sending her to the office for discipline was useless.

As a new teacher, she was still trying to get the hang of things, but she seemed to be spending more time disciplining a few rather than actually teaching the majority. Last week, she called the homes of two unruly boys from her third period class. The boys got mad at her and decided to give her telephone number to the entire class. She had to turn her ringer off before going to bed now because she was sick of being woken up by prank phone calls in the middle of the night. That would be the last time she ever called any students from her personal phone again. Mrs.

Johnson wondered what the repercussions would be if she called April's house and if it would even be worth all the trouble.

6

It was Sunday morning at Mt. Zion Baptist Church. Mary watched Pastor Zachariah Williams sitting down looking around as he rubbed his salt and pepper beard up in the pulpit from her regular post as an usher. He took in all of the faces in the sanctuary and balcony over the top of his reading glasses. Mary had finally convinced him that his new specs made him look distinguished. So now he kept them pushed down on his nose until he needed them instead of keeping them in his inside jacket pocket. She didn't understand how a man as fine as a frog's hair split four ways felt insecure about a little pair of eyeglasses.

Aside from a few pounds in his midsection and his gray hair, which she loved, he still looked as handsome as he did the first time she heard him preach twenty years ago in 1970. There were only about thirty people in attendance back when he began preaching. His humble beginnings was a far cry from the nearly fifteen hundred members they had today. The small choir had also grown to be one of the largest and best choirs in metro Atlanta in her opinion. Five years ago, through the money they raised in a building fund, they were even able to add on to the building.

Mary momentarily turned her attention to Zachariah's son Joshua who was standing in the pulpit. He was the assistant pastor, but he never seemed enthused about his position. "I would like for all the men to stand." Some men sprang up out of their seats. While others were slow to respond probably because they were unsure of what they were about to be asked to do. A few teenage boys, including Junior, looked puzzled wondering if the men of the church included them. Before Mary could motion for him to remain seated, he was up on his feet. She smiled that her grandson considered himself a man. If only she could get him to be more responsible at home. "How many of you have registered to attend our men's conference next month?" Only a few hands went up. Joshua enthusiastically continued, "We can do better than that men of Zion. I know you aren't going to let the women of Zion have a bigger conference than us again this year." That got a lot of giggles and mumbles from the female members. "Raise your hand if you need a registration card from one of our ushers." After she passed out a few registration cards, as one of the deacons made the church announcements, Mary let her mind wander back to her thoughts about Pastor.

Zachariah told her many stories about his family and friends being skeptical and warned him about building a church in the heart of the ghetto, but he did it anyway. Some of Zion's congregation did come from the struggling neighborhood. But the majority of the church members came from other nearby neighborhoods, like Buckhead or Decatur, even as far away as Alpharetta or McDonough.

Much of the growth had to be because Zachariah was a dynamic preacher who got even better with time. Spending countless hours with him over the years while she worked as a volunteer, showed Mary that he didn't just talk the talk. He also walked the walk. Zachariah was always doing something to help his congregation and the community. And he treated the poorest member of his congregation as well as he did the wealthiest. That's why she had been a faithful member of Zion from the very beginning.

She could also relate to him. They were both in their fifties and unfortunately they had each lost their spouses recently. Her husband had been gone a little over a year. Since she hated being alone in an empty house, Mary tried to spend as much time as possible at the church since then. By doing so, Zachariah helped her through one of the hardest times in her life. She didn't know what she would have done without him.

Then his wife passed away eight months ago. The first lady had been so diligently involved in helping her husband build up the church that she didn't notice the lump forming in her right breast. She had a mastectomy and went through months of painful chemotherapy. But her cancer spread beyond her breast. She suffered with her illness for nearly two years. God finally called her home to be in peace on Valentine's Day. Everyone genuinely missed the first lady's presence at the church.

Mary sighed and looked at Joshua, who was sitting down next to his father now. Joshua seemed to take his mother's death the hardest. Before she died, his sweet old-fashioned mother pressured him to make an honest woman out of one of the many females that he was rumored to be dating at the church. One day Mary overheard her yelling at him in his office," It really doesn't look right for the pastor's son at one of the most prominent churches in Atlanta, to also be one of the most eligible bachelors in the city." Next thing Mary knew, Joshua was engaged to a church member named Tracy. Mary had to hand it to Joshua, he picked the youngest prettiest one out of the bunch that she saw visiting him at his office on a regular basis.

The first family graciously offered to pay for the entire celebration since Tracy's family couldn't afford to pay for the wedding of her dreams. The first lady was just as excited about the wedding planning as her future daughter-in-law. It kept her mind off her illness. But from what Mary saw, Joshua acted like he was overwhelmed with his schedule at the church. He showed no desire to get involved in the wedding planning with them. In fact, Mary didn't see any desire concerning Tracy at all. Their engagement seemed to be more for appearances than for love. Mary looked at Tracy sitting on the front pew of the church and almost pitied her. Many women wanted to be in her spot, but the couple didn't look happy to her. If she were sitting on the front pew, she wouldn't have a fake smile like Tracy did.

Mary noticed that a lot of single women at the church wanted the first lady's position as well, now that Zachariah's wife was gone. Hordes of older women circled around like buzzards and then dove in to try and get their time with the grieving pastor who was unintentionally back on the market.

She couldn't help feeling a tinge of jealousy.

Not wanting to ruin her mood thinking about Zacharia showing attention to another woman, Mary turned her attention to the pew that held her grandkids. Brooklyn was on her feet clapping and singing along with the choir. "Trouble don't last always." Mary couldn't help but smile. She looked so adorable singing her heart out. Brooklyn was oblivious to her brother who was about to pull her hair. Anthony glanced over at Mary to see if the coast was clear. It wasn't, so he averted his eyes and dropped his arm as if he wasn't doing anything wrong. April chipped away her nail polish but Mary could see her mouth moving and her head bobbing up and down.

Mary knew April hated to sit with her siblings instead of going to teen church. But it was her own fault. When they first moved in with her, Mary wanted them to be with kids their own age at church. One Sunday she went to pick April up from the teen room and the volunteer confided in her that April tried to start a fight. Embarrassed, Mary looked at the female volunteer, then April, and back to her. She apologized profusely for her granddaughter's disrespectful behavior. That was the end of children's church for all of them.

A few more latecomers arriving caught Mary's attention. She put a smile on her face to greet them and showed them to some open seating. When it was time for Zachariah to preach, the ushers finally took their seats. Mary let out a sigh of relief and discreetly eased her heels off. But she had to wiggle her toes and do some pointing and flexing to try and get rid of the stiffness that had already set in. But her sore feet weren't going to distract her from listening to the best part of service.

After church, Mary watched Zachariah and Joshua stick to their normal routine of shaking the congregation's hands as they exited the sanctuary. Then they headed downstairs to the remodeled church basement to eat dinner with the members. The two handsome men, both six feet tall in nicely tailored suits, walked shoulder to shoulder across the hall and headed to the stairwell.

After a few steps Zachariah looked up at Mary and smiled. He asked, “Will I see you tomorrow?”

“Of course. I’ll be here bright and early.”

“Good.” He paused and stared at her as if he wanted to say something else.

Just then Joshua stopped walking and noticed his dad staring at Mary. From where she stood, Mary thought she noticed Joshua’s jaw clench.

“Dad, I’m hungry. Let’s go eat.”

To be a grown man, Joshua acted like such a spoiled little kid at times. Mary wondered if he was trying to keep his father away from all the women at the church or just her. Zachariah waved goodbye to Mary and the kids and proceeded down the stairs to catch up with his hungry son.

For years, Mt. Zion sold heaping dinner plates of fried chicken, collard greens, macaroni and cheese, and cornbread every Sunday. Mary thought the volunteers that missed service to cook in the kitchen did a good job. But no one could fry chicken that was crunchy on the outside yet tender on the inside as well as she could.

When Brooklyn asked, “Grandma, why can’t we get dinner from here too?”

“Never trust a skinny cook.” Mary laughed at her

own joke.

Brooklyn tilted her head to the side and looked up at her. “What does that mean Grandma?”

Mary rubbed her curvy hip and said, “Nothing baby. Forget I said that. Don’t worry. I’m gonna to cook us something delicious when we get home,” she assured her.

All of the women in the church kitchen were slimmer than Mary. Right then, she made it up in her mind to bring her own plate of food to Zachariah one day this week and show him what real soul food tasted like. They say the fastest way to a man’s heart is through his stomach.

7

"What about the park down the street?"

April's eyes got big. "Are you serious? Out in the open where everyone can see us?" She folded her arms across her chest.

"No." Brandon gently rubbed her arm. "I can find us a spot where no one will see what we're doing."

Still not convinced, April shook her head. "I don't know." She was trying to be a good girlfriend, but what he was asking her to do was bold even for her. So she made it a point not to look at his cute face or gaze into his hazel eyes or she would give in.

"Well you know we can't go to my house. We can't go to your house since you stay with your grandmother now." Now pointing at her he continued, "So you'd better think of something else then 'cause -."

April was getting annoyed now. She interrupted,

"Because what?" Was he really threatening her?

"I got needs. Do you know how many girls like me? It's not like I gotta beg or nothing." Since he hadn't persuaded her, suddenly he wasn't talking so sweet anymore.

Yes, she knew how many other girls wanted her boyfriend, but right now she didn't want to let on that she knew. "So what you trying to say?"

"Look, I'll talk to you later."

"Baby, wait a minute. We can figure this out."

Brandon slammed her locker, spun the dial, and started walking away. April tried to grab his arm but he jerked it out of her reach. She dropped her head then snuck a quick look to make sure that no one overheard their exchange or saw him leave her standing there looking stupid.

Not many boys wanted to be with a girl who got kept back in the eighth grade. April knew she was lucky to have Brandon. He was easily one of the finest boys in the school. And she was determined that she wasn't going to lose him because she couldn't keep him happy. If finding another place for them to keep having sex was what she had to do to keep him, she would figure out a way to do it.

Later on that day, once the bell rang for dismissal, her classmates rushed out of the room to catch their buses, be picked up or walk home. April headed to her locker to blend in. She made her move a few minutes later when she watched the teachers from this end of the hallway head towards the media center for their weekly faculty meeting from the bathroom where she'd been hiding.

April quickly snuck into Mrs. Johnson's classroom and waited. She sat in a chair in the corner of the room wringing her hands. The room was darker than usual with the shades closed, but she didn't dare turn the lights back on and draw any unwanted attention to herself. Every few minutes she gazed in the direction of the windows to make sure no one moving around outside could see her. Finally, the door swung open and Brandon closed it behind him.

Her heart was racing and she let out a sigh of relief that it was him who entered the room. "I didn't know if you were gonna come," she said hesitantly.

"The security guards were roaming the halls. I had to wait so I wouldn't get caught."

April didn't move from her chair.

He threw his arms up in the air and smiled. "So what's up? You left a note in the locker of where to meet you. I'm here now. You just gonna stay all the way over there in the corner?"

She stood up and took his hand leading him to her teacher's small supply room.

April and Brandon both jumped at the bright light that was turned on. Brandon stared at her with huge eyes but didn't move as if he wanted to act like they were invisible. So April wiggled and struggled to push him off of her to make him snap out of it. She watched Brandon jump up and turn his back to Mrs. Johnson trying to zip up his jeans as she fumbled to get up and fix her own clothes. Her heart was beating so fast but she could feel the tears about to fall from her eyes.

"April Lewis, get your fast behind up right now! When he finally turned around Mrs. Johnson recognized him and uttered, "Brandon Jackson." She looked back and forth between the two of them. "I can't believe that you two." The teacher closed her eyes and shook her head. When she opened them she continued her rant. "You shouldn't even be here. School is out, you should be at home."

Bringing her hand up to her face, April momentarily closed her eyes. When she opened them, Brandon looked like he was still trying to figure out what to do next. She picked up the two jackets that they had been using as their pallet and handed his back to him to avoid her teacher's eyes.

Her boyfriend finally got the courage to speak. "Mrs. Johnson, it's not what you think. We were just -."

But she put her hand up to cut him off and stated, "Save your explanation. I'm sure they would like to hear this in the office too."

April's eyes darted to her teacher. She crossed her arms across her chest, exhaled and said, "Don't waste your time Brandon. She's gonna send us to Mr. Brown's office anyway."

Mrs. Johnson smiled and answered, "You know what? I've tried it that way. I think I'll try something different today." She stepped to the side and ordered. "Let's go."

April raised an eyebrow. She wasn't in any hurry to find out what Ms. Johnson had in mind. The three of them walked side-by-side down the long hallway to the main office. All of a sudden, April felt so sick to her stomach she thought she would vomit before they reached the main office. She and Brandon stole nervous glances at each other during the walk. He seemed just as scared as she was. In less than a minute, they were face to face with the principal and assistant principal, who were just returning from the faculty meeting.

“Are you on your way to see us Ms. Johnson?” asked the principal.

“Yes, we are.”

Mr. Brown pulled a couple extra chairs in the principal’s office so that everyone could have a seat. Once everyone was seated, Mrs. Johnson announced, “I just found April and Brandon sprawled out on my storage closet floor having sex.”

They said, “What?” in unison. April noticed that all eyes were fixed on her like she’d been the only one on the floor. She rolled her eyes and then stole a glance at Brandon before crossing her arms over her chest and facing the adults again. Brandon was suddenly trying to play it cool like he was off the hook. At that moment, April didn’t know who she was more furious with. The three adults in the room who acted like she was the big bad devil and Brandon was a little innocent angel or her boyfriend who pressured her into this mess in the first place. It was true that he didn’t make frequent trips to the main office like she did. And he was much smarter than she was, but he was definitely not the saint they must have imagined him to be.

Mr. Brown wanted to know, “How did they get in your closet to begin with?”

Mrs. Johnson threw her head back and her eyes got big. But she quickly recovered and glared at him when she replied, “I guess I was so eager to get to the faculty meeting that I forgot to lock my classroom door.”

April watched the tense exchange between the two adults and was relieved that the attention was off of her.

Mrs. Johnson turned her head to the principal and asked, “So what are you going to do about these two?”

The principal turned to face them. “I won’t tolerate children behaving like this in my school. I am going to have to suspend both of you for five days.”

“Five days?” Brandon asked in a high-pitched voice. April noticed his hand twitching on his legs. “Can’t we just get in school suspension or something?” She hadn’t seen him act like this before. This was the total opposite of the cocky attitude he had earlier in the day at his locker.

“No. I’m afraid not,” she quickly replied. “Mr. Brown, take this young man to your office so he can call his parents and let them know what’s going on please.”

April tried to touch Brandon’s hand as he got up to let him know that everything was going to be alright, but he pulled his hand away. She watched him walk away in shock. *Why is he mad at me? What did I do?*

Once the two males left the room The principal picked up her telephone, selected a phone line, and held it out towards April for her to call home.

8

"Have you lost your mind little girl? I cannot believe I had to come up to your school because you think you're grown." Mary had been yelling at April since she stepped into the principal's office to get her. She only paused briefly outside when players of the football team stopped walking from the field to the building. Some of them even took off their helmets to listen. Watching the boys cover up their mouths and start laughing made her realize how loud she was.

In the car, she announced, "This ain't gonna be no vacation, honey. I'm going to work you until you drop." Mary turned to April to see if her words were sinking in. "You're going to scrub the bathroom from top to bottom, do the laundry, and clean the oven. Then you are going to wax the kitchen floor, reline my kitchen cabinets with contact paper, and rake the leaves in the yard. That's just what I can think of off the top of my head. Give me a little while to think about it and you might find yourself on a ladder cleaning the gutters or painting the house."

Mary noticed that April had the audacity to narrow her eyes as she stared back at her. "Grandma, I know you're mad that you had to come up here to pick me up, but you didn't have to embarrass me in front of everybody. It's hard enough to keep any friends since I got kept back. Everyone thinks I'm stupid."

"Embarrassing you?" Mary was beginning to lose her voice since she had been yelling so much. "There isn't anything that you can say to make me feel sorry for you. You were wrong and you know it. Embarrassing me by having sex in a closet at school. Don't you have any self-respect?"

"Can you just pull off? Everybody in the entire school doesn't need to know my business."

April did have a point. So, Mary pulled out of the parking lot before she continued. Plus, she had to slow down and catch her breath. Her grandchild had gotten her all worked up. "You need to be in your books learning reading and math so you can graduate instead of worrying about some rusty behind little boy."

April mumbled, "His behind ain't rusty." That smart remark got April backhanded across the face. Mary wanted to do more damage, but she had to keep both hands on the steering wheel. Her nostrils flared as she glanced over at April breathing hard and rubbing her cheek. Both of them were nearly in tears but for very different reasons.

"You are grounded, young lady. That means you won't be going anywhere, having company or talking on the phone until further notice."

When they arrived home, April stomped to the

bathroom and slammed the door. Mary yelled, "I told you about slamming doors in my house little girl!"

The phone rang a few minutes after Mary got in the house. She was relieved that it was one of her book club members and not one of April's friends, because she needed an adult to vent to. They discussed how this generation of kids was so different then when they were growing up. How they tried things so much younger these days. Her heart felt heavy when she said, "I wonder how long she has been having sex. Can you imagine them lying down on that dirty hard closet floor?" Her friend of ten years agreed that the entire situation was nasty.

This was the time that she usually called April into the kitchen to help her cook, but she didn't want to be near that girl right now. So, Mary cooked dinner for her family alone as she talked on the phone.

Her friends suggested that Mary think about having April talk to someone. She even advised her to take the teenager to an OBGYN and put her on birth control pills. But Mary didn't agree with that. "That's like telling her that it's okay to keep having sex."

"I know that it sounds crazy to take your grandchild to the doctor for birth control but think about it. She just showed you that she is sneaking around having sex anyway. You've got your hands full with the three of them Mary. Imagine if April came home pregnant one day. You don't know how long their mama is going to be in jail. That would just be another mouth for you to feed."

The thought of April getting pregnant was one of the first things that popped into her mind when she got the phone call earlier, but she was trying not to believe that it could happen again. It happened to her and Felicia when they were both teenagers. Surely God wouldn't let that happen to three generations in a row.

Mary knew that her friend meant well, but she was even more distraught after she got off the telephone than she was before. She yelled, "Come eat." All of a sudden, she didn't feel well. Barely touching her food, her stomach did flips as she watched the kids eat heartily. There was an uncomfortable silence in the kitchen until the phone rang again.

She let the kids enjoy dinner and got up to answer. The familiar recorded voice asked, "Collect call from Felicia Lewis. Will you accept the charges?"

Mary's eyes immediately fell on April as she replied, "Yes. I'll accept." April rolled her eyes but the younger Lewis kids were excited that their mother was calling. Mary knew that not only did they want to talk to her, but they knew she would tell their mom about April. And they still wanted to know why their big sister got suspended.

After they said hello to their mother, Mary made them excuse themselves from the dinner table. "Take your plates and go watch TV in the living room, but don't get any food on my carpet." Without hesitation the two grabbed their plates and eagerly rushed into the living room totally forgetting all about being nosey. They asked every night if they could eat dinner in the living room while they watched TV. But Mary always said no. Tonight, because April was in trouble again, they hit the jackpot.

Once Mary broke the news to Felicia she mumbled, "Are you serious? I can't believe that girl." She sighed and said, "Ma, put April on the phone please."

Mary handed April the telephone and sat back down. The kitchen was quiet while Mary waited for April to respond. She wished that she could hear what Felicia was saying to her on the other end.

April finally exhaled and said, “Well I’m on punishment now. But even if I wasn’t, Grandma doesn’t let me do anything. I can’t go anywhere with my friends or have company. So how else can I be with my boyfriend except to sneak and see him?”

Mary waited through another silence. *She doesn’t need to be worried about a boy. April needs to be worrying about getting out of eight grade this time around.*

“It’s not my fault that you messed up and we ended up here. We could all be at home chillin’ right now if you hadn’t been so stupid.”

Mary’s mouth fell open. She knew how resentful April was about having to move out of their apartment. But she couldn’t believe the way she was talking to her mother. She put her head down and pretended to cut up her dinner so April couldn’t see her expression. Deciding to sit back and let Felicia handle it would be the best thing to do right now.

April said a yes a couple times and a sorry that she clearly didn't mean. Finally, April handed her grandmother back the phone and stomped to her room. Mary waited until she was out of earshot. “Didn’t you tell them that you were getting evicted?”

She could hear the frustration in her daughter’s voice when she answered. “No. They don’t need to know about that yet. I’ll find us another place to stay when I get out.” She paused for a second. “Did you think more about helping me get out of here?”

Thinking that the car could be sold for bail money, Mary asked about it again. "What happened to the car the kid's daddy left you when he took off?"

Every time she tried to ask her about it, Felicia changed the subject or lied and said that she had to get off the phone. Tonight was no different. "Ma, they are making us get off the phones now. I'll call you back soon." Mary could only assume that she sold it for drugs but was too ashamed to admit it. Since Felicia had pawned a lot of their things, obviously to pay for drugs since she wasn't paying the rent, there wasn't much left of value in there. Last week, Mary got the key from April and hired the man from next door and his son to move the couch and everyone's bedroom sets out of the apartment for her before it got put out on the curb. Then she had the men put the stuff in her unfinished basement and cover it with plastic while the kids were at school.

Later on that night, Mary called Zachariah before it got too late. She apologized, "I'm so sorry that I had to call you at home Pastor, but I really need to talk to you."

He chuckled a little and said, "You know I don't mind when my favorite church member calls me. Now stop worrying and tell me what's wrong."

Mary told him most of the details of the day, leaving out the sleazy description of the storage closet floor. Saying only that April had been caught making out in the classroom with a boy. "She got herself suspended for five days and she tried to blame everyone else." She wiped away the tears from her eyes and continued, "When I talked to my friend, she advised me to take her to the doctor and get her on birth control. But I think that is just telling her that what she is doing is okay. What do you think?"

Zachariah sighed heavily and answered, "Our young people are trying to grow up so fast. Aren't they? I heard on the news that teen pregnancy is at an all-time high this year." Mary pictured him playing with the edges of his mustache like he usually did when he was thinking. "I don't believe in fornication, but if she is having sex anyway, you need to protect her. April probably looks at both of us like we are old as dirt and couldn't possibly understand her. So she won't talk to either of us, but maybe just maybe, she might sit down and talk to Joshua. He is older than her, but the young people look up to him. He might be able to talk some sense into her or at least help us figure out what to do next."

"It's worth a try. What do we have to lose?"

9

"Son, I need you to talk to April Lewis for me."

Joshua spun around in his chair to face his dad with a puzzled look on his face.

Zachariah walked further into his office and had a seat. "The school called Mary, because they caught April in one of the classrooms after school messing around with a boy. And you know how women are. Mary got herself all worked up talking about her winding up pregnant."

It wasn't often that his father walked down to his office. Usually he summoned Joshua to his office. He studied his father's demeanor and realized that this was important to him. "April isn't the only kid to get in trouble in the congregation Dad." He picked a pen up and tapped his forehead with it. "I'm curious why you need me to talk to her?" Joshua made sure that he put the emphasis on the word me.

"Well you know her mom is in jail and her dad ran off. You are her parents' age. I just thought that you could meet with her. Advise her. Be a kind of father figure to her. And find out where her head is at for us."

Joshua was taken aback. Had he heard what he thought he heard? He leaned forward and asked, "Us?"

"Yes, Mary and I." His dad answered him too nonchalantly for his liking. "She has her hands full taking care of these three kids."

Joshua leaned back in his chair. They were quiet for a minute. His dad was impatiently staring at him waiting for his answer. He even threw his hands up in the air and looked at him as if to say hurry up and answer me.

"Wow. You are really worried about her aren't you?"

"Of course I am. I worry about all my members."

A smirk appeared on Joshua's face. "Come on Dad. You know what I mean. She's not just any member. Is she?"

"Son, you're right." He paused like he was searching for the right words to say. "Mary helps out a lot around here. She is good to Mt. Zion so I want to be good to her and her family."

"So you want me to talk to her granddaughter for the good of the church?" Joshua asked to toy with his father.

Zachariah stood up and stared down at him. "Are you going to talk to her or not?"

The sides of Joshua's lips dropped. "Sure, Dad. I'll talk to her," he replied respectfully.

"Good. She will be here at 1:00 this afternoon," he announced over his shoulder as he exited the office.

Joshua pounded his fist on his desk. Once again his

father had talked him into doing something he didn't want to do. He came into his office asking him to see someone who he had already made an appointment for him to speak to. Why bother even asking him? "Unbelievable," he mumbled under his breath.

Joshua loved his father dearly, but he resented him too. His father and mother had chosen ministry as a way of life. He, on the other hand, was born into it. Since he was the first born, he was always told that Mt. Zion Baptist Church would one day be his. But Joshua didn't think this huge responsibility being thrust upon him was such a great prize.

Why couldn't he take a chance and pick what was behind curtain number two like people did on Let's Make a Deal? His father wouldn't have any part of it though. Growing up, every time he tried to venture out on his own in some way, his dad tightened the reins. Then his mom would make him feel guilty by saying something like, "How can you say no to God? He has a path set forth for us and we need to follow it."

He used to argue that his brother, the minister of music, would be a much better pastor than him. His mother argued back that music was his brother's passion so he needed to be with the choir and play the piano. Joshua remembered how he used to laugh at David and call him a sissy for playing the piano and taking weekly lessons when they were little. Now that they were older and the church responsibility was going to fall on him, not his brother, he kicked himself for not learning how to play an instrument himself.

Instead, he was trapped in a job that he didn't even

want. Stuck doing things for his dad and other people that he didn't want to do day in and day out. What in the world did he know about counseling a teenage girl? He didn't even like kids. Most of his friends that he went to high school with were married with a house full of kids by now. He had been a fool and let his mother pressure him into getting engaged, but he wasn't going to be tied down with a kid too. Changing diapers was not in his plan. He didn't see working at Mt. Zion for the rest of his life in his future either. This was his father's calling, not his. And his dad was going to find that out soon enough.

And if he didn't know any better, he would think that his dad was falling for Mary in a romantic way. She was a pretty woman for her age and she was full figured like his mom was. His parents were married forever and his dad was always very affectionate towards her, so Joshua concluded that his dad was attracted to curvy women. Mary didn't wear much makeup or dress too young for her age like some of the other women he noticed throwing themselves at his dad lately. Joshua wondered if she was just being a bit subtler about her approach. Mary had been a faithful member of the church for as long as he could remember. She had always been very sweet to all of them, not just his father. Still, other than his mother, Joshua didn't trust too many women.

His mom hadn't even been gone a year yet. It was way too soon to forget about her and move on. What was his father thinking? Besides, of all the available women at Zion why her? Mary was taking care of her three grandchildren, one of which seemed to be an aspiring juvenile delinquent. April would be their problem too if his father started dating her. He was stuck counseling her already. Just imagine if they became a couple. Joshua decided that he couldn't let his dad get serious about Sister Mary.

10

April tried unsuccessfully to sneak on the house phone and call Brandon before she went to bed. It was hard with three other people in the house. She wondered if he was trying to sneak and call her too.

Their relationship worked well because he had the freedom to call his parents and tell them that he was going over to a friend's house after school. They didn't seem to ask any questions. Since her mother was seldom home, he came over a couple times a week and hung out in her bedroom most of the time. April threatened the brats with bodily harm if they snitched on her when their mom finally came home.

Now that she lived with her grandmother, April was scared that she might lose him to a girl who had more freedom than she did. That's how she had ended up on the hard storage closet floor when he complained that they hadn't been able to sneak and have sex in weeks.

April laid in the bed trying to fall asleep but it was too early. Since her grandmother was so upset, she was sent to bed at the same times as the younger kids. Her grandmother really knew just how to get to her. In bed, Brooklyn kept asking her questions about why she got suspended but April wouldn't answer her.

"I bet you got into a fight, huh?" her sister prodded. "Nope, I bet you cursed out your teacher. Is that it, April? Is that what you did this time?"

April was very irritated with her grandmother, her mother, and now her little sister. So she shouted, "Just shut up and go to sleep."

It wasn't long before Brooklyn was snoring in her face, kicking her legs, and hogging all the covers. April couldn't stand sharing a bed with her nosy little sister. Her grandmother had a three-bedroom house. She didn't understand why she couldn't get a room to herself since she was the oldest. But her grandmother said her brother and sister were too old to share a room since they were the opposite sex.

After April laid in bed wide awake thinking for a couple hours, she decided that she wasn't going to wait a whole week to see Brandon again. As soon as her grandmother's back was turned, she was going to sneak off to see him.

The next morning, her grandmother came into their room and tried to quietly wake up her oldest grandchild without waking up the youngest one. She slid the covers off of her, shook her shoulder and whispered for April to get up. When that didn't work, she hollered, "April Lewis, get your behind out of that bed right now. I told you that this wasn't going to be a vacation. You've got work to do." When Brooklyn started rubbing her eyes she said, "I'm sorry baby. Go back to sleep for a little while."

April had nothing but contempt in her when she glared at her mean grandmother. She stomped her feet as she stormed past her headed towards the bathroom. Her grandma didn't ease up though. She continued outside the closed bathroom door, "Just use the bathroom and brush your teeth. You don't need to take a bath. You are about to get dirty doing some yard work."

After a few minutes of sulking, she quit stalling and came out of the bathroom. Her grandmother gave her a brick hard granola bar and instructed her to rake all of the leaves in the front and backyards. Then bag up all the leaves and put the bags at the curb. April thought that her twelve-year-old brother should be the one doing the yard work. She cursed her grandmother the entire time and tried to plan her escape. The only problem was she didn't have any money or any place to go.

Some of the kids at her middle school snuck and sold candy out of their book bags. Everyone knew who sold candy and their greedy customers kept them busy. April figured she could do the same. That would take care of her money problems.

When she finally finished with her back breaking yard work, her edges were frizzy and whatever curls she had in her hair this morning were flat. Her hands were red and sore from gripping the rake for hours. She was tired and even felt a little dizzy now that the sun was beating down on her. But for the life of her, she didn't want to give her grandma the satisfaction of seeing her suffer. So she sat outside on some cinder blocks and rested for a few minutes before going inside. Once April's breathing was back to normal, she wiped the sweat off her forehead and sauntered into the kitchen like she didn't have a care in the world.

Her grandmother didn't look up from spreading mayonnaise on wheat bread. She dryly ordered, "Go wash your hands for lunch." April did as she was told because she was starving. She came back to the table to eat hoping her grandmother wouldn't try to hold a conversation with her. Just as April started enjoying her sandwich she heard, "Girl, I didn't hear you say your grace."

April closed her eyes and put her head down pretending to say her grace to get her grandmother off her back. But what was she thanking God for? In her opinion, she had a crappy life. If God was so good, then why had her father left them? Why did He let it break her mother's heart so much that she changed? If God was so amazing, then why did He let her mom get addicted to crack? What kind of God gave you nice things and then takes them all away from you piece by piece? And why would He let family that was supposed to love each other stop speaking to one another? If He loved her so much, then why wouldn't he make her as smart as her little sister so that she could graduate from middle school? Why would He put her mother in jail and leave them to fend for themselves? And why would God send the one person that didn't want her to rescue her?

She kept thinking that if her daddy came back, he could fix everything. He would have enough money to bail her mom out of jail and get her a great lawyer to win her case. Her mom wouldn't be depressed anymore so she would stop doing drugs cold turkey because her man was back. Daddy would move back to their old apartment or an even better place. They would have money again and replace everything their mom pawned while he was gone. He would rescue her from her strict grandmother. And things could go back to normal.

But for now, the two of them sat in silence as they ate. April assumed that she was finished with chores for the day. She gasped when her relentless grandmother demanded, "Wash the breakfast dishes."

April noticed the pans on the stove and protested, "But I didn't even get to eat breakfast. Why do I have to wash everyone else's mess?"

"Because I said so." Those must have been her grandmother's favorite words.

Her grandmother left her alone in the kitchen mumbling under her breath to a sink full of suds in the double sink. A few minutes later she returned to the kitchen with an announcement. "I forgot to tell you that you have a one o'clock appointment with Joshua Williams at the church."

April's eyes got big. She swung around to face her grandmother, "Why do I have an appointment with the pastor's son?"

"Don't be disrespectful. He is the assistant pastor of the church and he wants to talk to you about your behavior. So hurry up and get ready."

11

April and her grandmother arrived at the church and knocked on Joshua's office door exactly at one o'clock. She sat quietly stewing as the two adults spoke. *Why do I have to talk to this man? He ain't my daddy.*

After a few minutes of small talk, Mary excused herself from the room. With a big grin on her face she stated, "Well, I guess I will go see what work Pastor has for me to do this afternoon." Once she was up, Mary looked down at her grandchild and ordered, "Stop looking so evil and talk to Pastor Joshua."

At first the two of them sat in complete silence and listened to Mary's high heel shoes click down the hallway. Joshua broke the ice by saying, "I hear that it's been rough for you lately April."

April sat there staring at the floor nodding her head

in agreement but didn't speak.

"First your dad leaves you. Then your mom was taken away from you. And then you had to move out of your home and into your grandmother's. All of that was out of your control." He paused for a few seconds. "It's okay if you look at me. I don't bite."

April exhaled and folded her arms in front of her when she slowly lifted her head.

"Then your boyfriend and you get caught in a private moment which got you suspended from school." He made a small gesture by turning his hand upward and laying it back down. "You did have control over that happening though." He chuckled a little. "And now you got dragged into my office. I bet that you think everyone is ganging up against you."

April didn't know what to make of Pastor Joshua yet. She was just relieved that he wasn't preaching scriptures to her.

"I want you to play a game with me." Joshua stopped talking and looked directly into April's eyes to make sure that she was paying attention. She stared at him suspiciously. He said, "I'm serious. Are you ready?"

April nodded.

"Imagine that you are a fifty something year old lady," he said.

April giggled picturing herself that old. She replied, "I don't know if I want to live that long."

Joshua smiled again and said, "Sure you do. Okay so you live alone in your own house because your husband passed away and your daughter is grown."

She was looking up at the ceiling imagining until he

said that. Then she realized he wanted her to imagine herself as her grandmother. Frowning, April kept playing his game anyway.

"You thought that you raised your child right and had three beautiful grandkids. You and your daughter have had your differences, but you still love her. The two of you hadn't talked for a while and then one day you get a call saying that she is in jail," he paused for a second. "How would you feel, April?"

April sighed and answered, "I dunno. Guess I would be worried about everyone."

Joshua agreed, "Of course you would. "He continued, "So you try and do the right thing like God teaches us to do. You go and get your grandchildren, right?"

She nods.

"You're thinking everything is going to be alright, thinking they will be happy to spend long overdue time with their grandmother who loves them with all of her heart. Then you realized that only two of them are happy to see you. The third one doesn't want you to lead her in the right direction or even try to take care of her. She is making bad decisions and is mad at the world. And you are the one she is taking it out on."

April interrupted, "I'm not mad at the world."

Joshua shook his finger and said, "Remember you are a fifty something year old woman."

She popped her lips and exhaled.

He continued, "You try everything that you know how to do. You take her to church, try and talk to her, try, and show her that you love her, and most of all you set boundaries for her because she needs discipline. But it's not working, so what do you do April?"

April smiled about the answer she came up with. She announced, "I would leave her alone and let her do what she wanted to do."

He nodded, "Oh okay. If she wanted to set herself on fire, would you let her?"

April sighed. "Uh-unh."

"Well what if she was doing something else that you knew from experience would hurt her? Would you let her do it?"

April paused because she knew that this was a trick question. She wanted to come up with the correct answer to win his stupid game.

Joshua cautioned, "Remember, this is your grand baby and you love her."

She reluctantly gave in. "I guess I would try to stop her."

Joshua smiled. He emphasized every word when he said, "Well that is exactly what your grandmother is trying to do for you. You've got your whole life ahead of you to worry about boys. Right now, you should be worrying about school. It wasn't that long ago that I was your age. You think your grandma is tough? Imagine growing up a preacher's kid. I couldn't do anything." He leaned in and lowered his voice. "Don't tell them I told you this, but I used to sneak around with my girlfriends too."

April smiled at Joshua and leaned closer too. "Really?"

"Look," he put his hands up to squelch her excitement. "Now that I'm older I understand why we shouldn't have been doing that. We could have gotten into the kind of trouble that we weren't old enough to handle. But I was a typical boy. And at that age, all guys think about is sex. Trust me. They will say whatever they have to say to get it."

April stopped smiling. She thought about how mean Brandon usually was. But when he wanted something from her all the sweet talking began. By the end of her talk with Pastor Joshua, April reluctantly agreed that she would leave boys alone for now and focus on school. Her impression of him had totally changed. He walked around looking handsome in a suit and tie but he wasn't uptight like he appeared on Sunday mornings. To April's surprise, he turned out to be pretty cool. *Grandma can punish me by making me come talk to him anytime.*

Mary and April rode home in silence later that afternoon. The suggestion that the assistant pastor gave about her grandmother knowing what was best for her stuck with April that night while she happily helped her grandmother cook dinner. For the short time that she was in the kitchen helping her grandmother cook, her grandma was actually nice to her.

"My mama never really showed me how to cook. We ordered take out a lot," April confessed.

Her grandmother shook her head. "Your mama never did like helping me in the kitchen. Burned her arm once on the oven door and that was it for her and cooking. But she sure loved to eat."

April smiled. "Yep, that's true."

They were quiet for a minute. Then her grandmother continued, "Your grandfather loved my cooking. I like cornmeal on my fish and he liked flour. So I used to mix the two together as a compromise. I still do it like that even though he's not here anymore."

April stared at her grandmother and sensed her getting sad. So she kept talking to keep that from happening.

"Grandma, how do I know if the grease is hot enough?"

"Oh, that's easy. Drop a tiny piece of the fish in there. If it starts sizzling right away then it's ready." She rubbed April's back and said, "Now don't forget to keep stirring those grits. I'm going to sit down and let you do it by yourself."

The house began to fill up with the aroma of fried catfish, cheese grits and flaky biscuits. April was proud of her first solo meal when she was done.

"Come eat," Grandma yelled. "Fish doesn't taste good when it's cold."

During dinner Brooklyn remarked, "Grandma, this is really good."

"Your sister cooked it."

April held her breath and waited for the smart comments to roll off the tongues of her siblings, but they didn't. They were too busy chewing and licking their fingers. April turned to her grandmother who gave her a wink and a smile.

After dinner, April kept Pastor Joshua's advice in mind when she had to wash dishes alone. A big chunk of it was forgotten when she was sent to bed with her little sister again. The next day when her grandmother made her upset by waking her up at the crack of dawn again, his wisdom vanished from her memory bank all together.

12

On Friday night, April laid in bed waiting for everyone else to fall sound asleep. She didn't care anymore what she promised Pastor Joshua the other day. Tonight, she was going to sneak out of the house to see Brandon. A friend of his from school was having a party and April knew that he wouldn't miss being there.

By ten o'clock, her grandmother was snoring in her room with a book on her lap. For the first time, April was happy that her grandmother made everyone in the house go to bed early. April eased out of bed hoping that her nosy little sister wouldn't wake up and catch her leaving. She put on her shortest pair of blue jeans shorts. They were so short she didn't dare wear them around her grandmother. If she bent over, anyone looking would get an eye full. And the wife beater she wore hugged her just right as well.

She slowly opened her bedroom door so that it wouldn't make any noise. She tiptoed down the long hallway into the kitchen without a sound until the floor right in front of the back door creaked. April froze. A few seconds later, she glanced over her shoulder and waited to see if her grandmother would come out into the hallway. When she didn't, April cautiously opened and closed the door behind her. As soon as her feet hit the ground she took off running away from the house as fast as she could.

It was late. Deep down, she knew that she had no business being out walking the streets of Atlanta in this neighborhood. But she had to see her man. Her heart started beating fast when she saw a group of shadows on a porch a couple house ahead. When she got a little closer, she was drawn to the way the funny cigarettes they were smoking smelled. So she tried to inhale it. One of the tall shadows turned up a beer bottle while walking off the porch to the bottom of the steps. "Hey baby girl, can I walk with you?"

April acted like she didn't hear him and started walking even faster after that. A few houses down, she turned to make sure that the shadow wasn't following her. She exhaled a huge sigh of relief that he wasn't.

It took her almost thirty minutes to walk to the house party. The first place April headed once she arrived was the bathroom next to the side door that she entered. Her bottom lip dropped and her eyebrows wrinkled when she looked in the mirror. In her rush to get to the party, she had sweated out the curls she put in her hair earlier in the day. There wasn't much she could do about it now except wipe the sweat off of her forehead, pull her hair back in a short ponytail like that's the look she chose for tonight, and apply the lipstick she squeezed in her front pocket just in case she needed it.

She left the bathroom and headed downstairs to the basement to begin her search. As she reached the bottom of the stairs, April caught a whiff of the musty basement from everyone's body heat. It took her eyes a few seconds to get used to the dimness of the room. She noticed a few of the guys admiring her as if she were fresh meat. Spotting a couple of her boyfriend's buddies, she walked in their direction. "Hey. Where's Brandon?"

They eyed each other and shrugged their shoulders and kept talking to each other. She got the impression that she was bothering them so she kept moving. When she turned the corner to enter the next room, she found her boyfriend hugged up in the dark corner of the room whispering in another girl's ear.

The unfamiliar girl sitting on his lap had a long ponytail weave hanging down her back and a face full of flawless makeup. She wore a low-cut t-shirt with a tight pair of jeans and had a new pair of Nike sneakers on her feet. The stones on her big hoop earrings glistened all the way across the room. She was everything that April was not. The girl was staring back at April. Finally Brandon looked up and eyeballed April too. April swore she saw his body jump.

She crossed her arms and glared at him. Brandon should've pushed the chick off him, jumped up and told her, "Babe, it's not what you think." Instead he started whispering in the heifer's ear again which made her giggle. His new girl turned her attention from April and whispered back in his ear which made him smile.

Doesn't she know that's my man? April wanted to

pull out the girl's fake hair and repeatedly punch her in her perfect little face. But she quickly realized that the two lanky girls flanked on both sides of her looked just like long ponytail girl were staring at her too, like they were her bodyguards. Realizing that she was outnumbered, she turned around and headed for the exit. The same two friends that lied and said that they didn't know where Brandon was were watching her with grins on their faces. Humiliated, she walked past them as quickly as she could.

Tears rolled down her cheeks as soon as she stepped back outside. And they kept falling for several blocks. But her sadness turned into anger on her lonely walk back home. She tried to remember Brandon being all over her in public like that but she couldn't remember a time when he was. The realization that all of their cuddling had been done in private, where no one could see them, infuriated her. *So that's what kind of girl he likes and wants to be seen with?*

She wished that her grandmother would take her to get a weave like that. Even a bad weave was better than no weave at all she reasoned. How could she compete with all those girls swinging their store-bought hair around the boys all day? Not to mention the cute clothes and the one-hundred-dollar sneakers. April knew exactly how much they cost because she had admired them in the mall the other day. If her daddy was still around, she would ask him to buy them for her. And he would do it too. He used to give her everything that she asked for to make her happy. But now she was stuck with someone who never let her have anything that she wanted.

As if her night wasn't horrible enough, when she slid her key in the lock and gently opened the back door, her grandmother shouted, "Where have you been?" She nearly peed on herself and cursed expletives under her breath. *I can't believe this. I'm never getting off punishment*.

"Did you hear me? I asked you where you've been, little girl." Slowly, her grandmother rose from the table where she had been drinking a cup of coffee.

April looked over her shoulder back at the door. For a second she thought about making a run for it. But she knew that she didn't have anywhere to go. She tried to pull her shorts down her thighs a little, took a deep breath and exhaled. "I just went to a party right down the street for a minute Grandma. I'm sorry." Then she braced herself in case she got backhanded again.

"You're just sorry that you got caught." Mary stood there staring her up and down for a few very uncomfortable seconds, that felt like hours, before she shook her head and walked away leaving April standing there with her head down.

13

As much as she hated school, when her five-day suspension was up, April was happy to be let out of the house to go back. She felt like she was the prisoner and her grandmother was the warden ever since she got caught sneaking back in the house from the party. Every single move she made; her grandmother was there to watch her make it. She couldn't be in a different room without her grandmother constantly checking to see what she was doing.

As soon as April walked in Mrs. Johnson's class for homeroom, she heard, "Oh no, she's back." The entire class started laughing. She stopped walking to her desk and just stood there examining the room. All thirty desks were filled with students. She balled up her fists at her side ready to defend herself, but she couldn't tell which boy in the back of the classroom disguised his voice to say it. April glanced at her teacher. Mrs. Johnson tried to hide it with her indifferent look on her face, but April could tell that she wasn't pleased about her being back either. So she lowered her head and kept walking to her desk.

She had more important things to worry about anyway. Although she had witnessed her boyfriend cuddled up with another girl at the party, April was convinced that once they were around each other again she could win him back. But when she went to her locker between classes, she was disappointed to see that Brandon had moved his things out. Then at lunch time, her so-called boyfriend walked past her table as if he didn't even see her. She got up to catch up with Brandon and grabbed him by his arm, "Oh so you don't know me now?"

Brandon yanked it away and warned, "Don't pull on me like that, shorty." He looked her square in the eyes and said, "I thought you would've figured it out the other night. You ain't worth all the trouble that you put me through. I've got somebody better than you now." He kept a straight face until they heard one of his crew chuckling. A smirk appeared on his face after the confession then he walked away towards his smiling friends.

April finally had to admit to herself what everyone else obviously knew, it was over. She fought hard to keep from blubbering on her humiliating walk back to her lunch table. "I thought that you and Brandon broke up," an inquiring classmate commented. "I saw him at a party with someone else the other night."

She was too embarrassed to manage more than, "Mind your own business."

By the time she got back to Mrs. Johnson's

classroom for Language Arts, she was angry. When she tried to get down the aisle to her desk, Tiffany was blocking the aisle. April yelled, "Would you move?"

Tiffany didn't say anything. She just kept trying to get the bulky book that was stuck out of her desk. April was already fuming about Brandon dumping her in the middle of the cafeteria and Tiffany wasn't getting out of her way fast enough to suit her. So April walked down the row anyway bumping into Tiffany causing her to fall backwards as April's backpack hit her in the face.

Mrs. Johnson was writing on the board with her back turned to her students. Her class was always hyper and made a lot of noise when they came back from lunch so April assumed that she usually tuned them out. On her way to her desk, April turned around in time to watch Tiffany run up to Mrs. Johnson wailing and covering her eye. "Can I go to the bathroom Mrs. Johnson?"

Startled, Mrs. Johnson stammered, "Of course. What's wrong?" But Tiffany ran out of the room crying hysterically without answering her teacher.

Mrs. Johnson looked to her students for answers. The class immediately started pointing and yelling. "April hit her in the head," was what she could decipher from the room full of kids all chiming in at the same time.

"Mrs. Johnson, April walked on her."

"She wasn't doing anything. April just knocked her down for no reason."

April watched as their teacher shook her head in disbelief at her class. "What?" She turned to April and yelled, "You haven't even been back a full day and you are already at it again?"

"I walked past her and my bookbag must have hit her." The teenager plopped down in her desk and folded her arms across her chest. "Why are you mad at me? She should have moved out my way."

Mrs. Johnson quickly sent one of her students to get the assistant principal. She paced the floor and tried to calm her students down. A few minutes later, she sent a different student to check on Tiffany in the bathroom. When the student finally returned she said, "The girl's bathroom was empty, Mrs. Johnson. I don't know where she is."

The students finally sat down and feigned reading their assignment in anticipation of what was to come. April sat glaring at Mrs. Johnson as she sat on the edge of her desk tapping her foot waiting for reinforcements. Apparently too anxious to sit still she finally opened the classroom door to look down the hallway to see if Mr. Brown was headed her way yet. Suddenly, Tiffany appeared at the threshold with her mother in tow. Mrs. Johnson instinctively stepped back when she saw the angry mother's fixed stare on her. April heard her say, "Whoa." A nervous grin spread across her face as she looked from Tiffany's bruised and swollen face to her mother's and back at her class. She slowly stepped out into the hallway and closed the door to talk to them in private.

The students were so quiet that you could hear a pin drop so they could make out what was going on in the hall. The irate mother shouted, "My daughter called me crying saying that this April girl is still picking on her. Luckily, we live right down the street. So I rushed up here to see what was going on for myself." Some kids started whispering. Others looked back at April with their hands over their mouths.

Someone whispered, “Shut up. I can’t hear.”

Tiffany's mother screamed, “I’m sick of my daughter coming home telling me about what this older girl April did to her. I’ve always taught her not to use her size to intimidate people, but I never meant for her to let them walk all over her.” She stopped venting for a second. A couple kids pointed to another shadow appear under the door.

The heavyset mother sounded even angrier now when she announced, “Now, I’m telling my child in front of you and him to knock April upside her head with a desk if she has to the next time she messes with her. If she doesn’t I will, since no one else around here will get off of their behinds to help her.”

They could hear Mr. Brown trying to calm the woman down. “Ma’am, I understand that you are upset, but -”

She interrupted him, “I don’t understand why these bad ass kids are mixed in with smart kids like my daughter anyway. Isn’t that girl supposed to be in high school?”

“Ma’am, why don’t we discuss your concerns in my office down the hall?”

The disgruntled mom snapped. “I don’t want to discuss my concerns with you anymore. Everyone around here acts too high and mighty for me. Maybe I will discuss my concerns with the police and press charges against this April girl. And maybe I’ll get a lawyer and sue the school for not protecting my child from a bully.” Before Mrs. Johnson or Mr. Brown could respond, two of the shadows disappeared.

“What happened here, Mrs. Johnson?”

"I was writing on the board so I didn't see it, Mr. Brown. But the students said that Tiffany wasn't doing anything but putting a book in her desk when April ran into her and her backpack hit her in the face."

The kids could hear his heavy sigh from inside the room. "I'm putting April on in-school suspension."

The class got riled up again. Everyone knew about ISS. Students had to do nonstop class work from the beginning of the school day until the end of the day. The kids were not allowed to leave the room and interact with any of the other students at the school. The room was equipped with a restroom and cafeteria lunches were brought to the room so they could eat at their desks. The six foot three-inch-tall well-built black male basketball coach in charge of in school suspension was mean and very intimidating so the kids hated him.

Mr. Brown swung the classroom door open. A couple of kids got busted trying to listen in and scrambled back to their seats. He ignored the scattering students, found the face in the crowd that he was looking for and demanded, "April, I need to see you in my office now." He then instructed Mrs. Johnson to fill out an incident report and leave it in his mailbox by the end of the day.

Mrs. Johnson stepped back into her room and closed the door once April and Mr. Brown were gone. April could hear one of the boys loudly mimicking Tiffany's mom, "Knock April upside the head with a desk if you have to." The rest of the class busted out laughing.

April couldn't believe that she was in trouble again. Her life was falling apart around her. She felt like her grandmother had hands around her neck and she couldn't breathe. Her boyfriend was squeezing her heart, breaking it into little pieces. And now Mr. Brown had her butt in a sling. Five days of in school suspension was just as bad as her grandmother's prison at home. She wanted it all to stop.

Mr. Brown told her grandmother the only reason he gave her in school suspension this time was because he didn't want her to miss so much school that she was in jeopardy of failing the eighth grade again. While the adults talked, April thought to herself that she would drop out of school before she got kept back again.

When she arrived home she had to listen to her grandmother rant and rave once again before she could finally hide out in the bathroom. She locked the door behind her, turned the water on in the tub full blast, and flushed the toilet so that no one could hear her wailing. After about an hour of soaking in the tub and feeling sorry for herself, Anthony started banging on the bathroom door. "April, when are you coming out of there? I have to use it."

April hollered, "Good. I hope you pee on yourself then." She heard a loud kick on the door that nearly made her jump out of the water.

Then she heard him stomping down the hall hollering, "Grandma, April won't get out of the bathroom."

April rolled her eyes, let the water out of the tub and dried off. Looking at herself in the mirror over the sink she was disappointed as usual. She opened the medicine cabinet to find a Q-Tip for her ears but got distracted by her grandmother's medicine bottles. Some were vitamins. The others were prescriptions that had not been finished. She grabbed a handful of the prescriptions, put them in her pants pocket, and headed for her bedroom.

At dinner, everyone was talking and laughing except April. All she could think about was all of the things she had done with Brandon yet he dumped her anyway. She was tired of constantly being chastised by her grandmother so she got up and started washing the dirty dinner dishes before she was even finished eating to avoid hearing her mouth. Too tired to fight with her siblings over the living room TV, April went to bed early to be alone.

April was trying hard to wake up out of her fog. For some reason someone was shaking her by her shoulders and yelling her name repeatedly. She was so groggy it was difficult to focus. Finally able to open her eyes, she slowly eased up out of the bed recognizing that it was her grandmother's holding on to her arm. But as soon as she stood all the way up, like she was being instructed to, her body gave way and she hit the floor with a loud thud almost pulling her grandmother down with her. She struggled to move her hand up to her forehead because it suddenly felt like it was on fire.

Her grandmother started screaming, "Oh my God! Oh my God!" Then she ran off and everything was suddenly quiet again.

14

The digital alarm clock on his nightstand read twelve thirty A.M. when Zachariah's sleep was interrupted by the loud ringing of his phone. Even in his groggy state, he could recognize Mary's voice on the other end. He quickly sat straight up when he realized that she was crying.

"Pastor, I'm at the hospital about to lose my mind. April tried to kill herself by taking a bunch of my pills. The doctors are in there pumping her stomach now." She paused and took a deep breath to try and calm down. "Can you come down to Grady and wait with me please?"

"I'm already out of bed and halfway dressed. I'll get there as quickly as I can." He knew that with the hospital's reputation for being overcrowded and slow, it was going to be a very long night. But he didn't mind doing anything for Mary even if it was the middle of the night. She was always bending over backwards to help him as well.

Even on a weeknight there wasn't an empty seat in Grady Memorial Hospital's waiting room, but Zachariah spotted Mary right away in the crowd. She had on a short beige raincoat, she must have thrown on as an afterthought on her way out the door, over her emerald green two-piece pajamas with matching emerald house shoes and a multicolored silk scarf tucked behind her ears covering her shoulder length hair. He knew that she wouldn't be caught dead outside her house with her pajamas on under normal circumstances. But she still looked beautiful to him in her attire even with no makeup or jewelry on. When he got closer and saw the worried look on her face, he wanted to be the one to take all her pain away.

Mary stopped pacing back and forth between the rows of chairs when she noticed him walk in. She greeted him with a big hug. He whispered in her ear, "Don't you worry; the Lord isn't ready for her yet. He's got big plans in store for her future."

"Oh, I sure hope you are right. I should have thrown those bottles out a long time ago. I don't even remember what that medicine was for. Anyone of my grand babies could have taken them at any time. That was so stupid of me." She released him and wiped the corner of her eyes.

He shook his head and rubbed his hand up and down her arm. "You know that this is not your fault. If it hadn't been your pills, it could have been something worse."

Mary closed her eyes and leaned in for another supportive hug.

A little while later, a nurse came to escort Mary to see April. Zachariah followed closely behind them. The nurse reported, "We pumped her stomach and she should be back to normal soon. We checked the labels from the bottles you brought in. Luckily, the medicine had been expired for some time. But it's good that you rushed her here."

When they entered the cold room, April looked horrible. She was lying curled up in the hospital bed in the fetal position. The hospital staff left a big trash can next to her bed in case she needed to throw up again. Mary was quiet like she didn't know what to say. She just twisted the used tissue that she held in her hands. So Zachariah tried to break the silence by asking, "How are you feeling, April?" As soon as the words left his mouth he realized that it was a stupid question, but it was too late to take it back.

Without making direct eye contact she mumbled, "I'm okay." Then she closed her eyes, pulled the white sheets up, and tried to block them out.

The two adults stood side by side next to the hospital bed quietly watching April. Zachariah knew that the light above the bed was too bright for April to fall asleep, but they didn't bother her. He reasoned that she was probably feeling sad or embarrassed and wanted to be left alone.

A few minutes later, a young white doctor entered the room and asked Mary to step out in the hallway so they could talk. April's eyes opened, but when she saw that her pastor was still standing there staring at her, she quickly closed them. Zachariah couldn't help but chuckle. Then he patted April on her shoulder and said, "You are going to be just fine, young lady."

A minute later, hearing the door squeak, he noticed Mary quietly gestured for him to come join her in the hallway. Zachariah could see the doctor walking away heading into another patient's room. So he turned his attention back to Mary. She whispered, "The doctor said that if she was an adult that they would automatically keep her for a seventy-two-hour observation in the psychiatric ward. Since she is a minor, they are letting me take her home. But he recommended that April go see a psychologist and maybe even start taking an antidepressant."

The worry lines on her forehead let Zachariah know how she felt about the situation. He rubbed her arm again and advised, "Let's just get her home and into bed for now. You can decide what you want to do once you've had some rest." Suddenly realizing that the other two kids weren't with them, he asked, "Are Anthony and Brooklyn still at home in bed?"

Mary quickly looked at her watch. "Yes. I didn't want to drag them out in the middle of the night so I just told them that their sister was sick and to go back to bed. I promised them that I would be back home by the time the alarm clock went off for them to go to school."

"Well let's try to get out of here so you can keep that promise."

When it was finally time to leave, Zachariah left out first to get his car. The cold morning air hit his face when he stepped out the hospital's sliding glass doors. Despite the patient whining that she felt fine, the discharge nurse insisted that April had to be pushed down the hall out of the hospital in a wheelchair. Mary smiled when Zachariah pulled up to the curb and opened the car doors for them like a gentleman. April jumped out of the chair without looking back to thank her escort. Mary graciously apologized and thanked the uniformed man by shaking his hand before getting in the front passenger seat.

Everyone quietly enjoyed the ride home in his warm car. When they pulled into the driveway, it was still dark outside, but the sun would be coming up soon. The two adults walked behind April into the house. When they tucked her in bed, Zachariah whispered a brief prayer over her being careful not to wake Brooklyn up. Then Mary walked her old friend to the front door and said, “Thank you so much for coming to the hospital, Pastor. I don’t know what I would have done without you.”

He smiled and said, “Don’t mention it.” After a couple seconds he asked, “Let me ask you something. Is this about that boy again?” Mary explained that April had gotten into trouble on her first day back at school for attacking a girl she didn't like.

“Joshua and I will come talk to her later on today. We’ve got to get to the root of her issues,” he said. “We can’t have your grand baby feeling sad and taking her own life.” As Zachariah gave Mary a goodbye hug, he said, “I want you to try and get a little sleep. Okay? I’ll be back later this afternoon.”

Alone in his car on the drive home, Zachariah couldn’t help but shake his head. Mary was a God-fearing woman and was trying to live her life right. But he didn’t think that she was going to be able to handle April alone. He made a silent commitment to help Mary out as much as he possibly could. Then he prayed for the entire Lewis family before he laid down at home to try and go back to sleep himself.

Part Two
If You Can't Run with the Big Dogs, Stay on the Porch

15

Mary walked around her quiet house yawning while watering plants before she cooked breakfast for everyone. Ever since her grandkids moved in she felt like it was her duty to send them off to school with a hot meal in their bellies even if some days it was simply oatmeal. She knew that a lot of the young mothers let their kids eat breakfast at school. But she couldn't imagine any cafeteria cooking as well as she could. They couldn't cook sausage, grits with melted cheese, bacon, waffles, or pancakes like she did. She heard that the cafeteria's scrambled eggs were powdered and the butter wasn't even real.

Quietly, she woke up her two youngest grandkids for school. She planned to let April sleep a little while longer. Over breakfast the curious kids asked about their older sister. Brooklyn asked, "What's wrong with April Grandma? Why did she have to go to the hospital in an ambulance last night?"

Their grandmother's answers were intentionally vague. "Your sister is fine. She just needs to rest."

They turned to each other as if trying to communicate by mental telepathy. Anthony Jr. spoke up next. "Well maybe we should stay home too and help you take care of her."

Mary smiled at their cute attempt to have a day off and replied, "No, y'all can't stay home. Now hurry up and eat so you won't be late for school."

Brooklyn sighed, but then gulped down her food and ran to the only full bathroom in the house first.

As tired as she was, Mary couldn't fall asleep after the kids boarded their buses. She tossed and turned, feeling silly being in bed since the sun was shining brightly through the windows. Felicia was on her mind. It seemed like every time she called collect from jail, there was bad news to tell her about April. How was she going to explain to her child that they had almost lost one of the kids on her watch?

Felicia was locked up and couldn't do a thing to help from there. It was all up to Mary to protect April from herself. She knew that April was going to hate her and would fight her all the way, but so be it. She had to do what she had to do. Maybe when April got older she would thank her.

"No sense in wasting time lying in bed when I can't go to sleep any way," she mumbled as she got up and slid on her comfy house shoes. First thing she did was tip toe into her granddaughters' room and check on April. Mary quietly watched the flower printed comforter heave up and down as

April snored away.

When the house phone rang, Mary quickly answered so the ringing wouldn't wake her up. The familiar voice on the other end of the phone cheerfully answered, "Good morning, Mary. It's Zachariah. Did you get some rest?"

"Good morning Pastor. I never did fall back to sleep. Too much weighing on my mind I guess. I've been thinking that I may have been too strict with April. Maybe I need to give her a little more freedom since she is a teenager. I don't know."

"We'll figure it out together Mary."

"Okay," she let out a sigh of relief because she liked to hear the word together roll out his mouth so easily. "I called her school and told them she was going to be absent today. I even held on to talk to Mrs. Johnson since she sees her twice a day for homeroom and Language Arts. Now that that is done, I'm going to sit here and read my book and drink some coffee. And I'm just gonna let April sleep until she wakes up on her own."

"That sounds good. Joshua and I will be over around eleven o'clock, if that's alright with you."

Mary smiled. "That's perfect. I'll see you then." She was grateful to have a pastor that cared about her and her troubled family at a time like this.

When April woke up and entered the kitchen she didn't even acknowledge her sitting there. Mary was enjoying Disappearing Acts, the latest novel by a new author named Terry McMillan. She overlooked her rudeness and announced, "The pastor and assistant pastor want to come by and check on you."

April's mouth dropped as she swung around from the

refrigerator to address her grandmother. "Can't you just call them and tell them that I'm okay?" Mary raised her eyebrow and looked at her like she was crazy. April must have realized that they were coming over whether she liked it or not. So she stumped out of the kitchen without getting any breakfast and Mary didn't say a word. She decided to give her some space. If she got hungry enough, she would be back.

At eleven o'clock on the dot, the doorbell rang. Mary was positive that it was her two anticipated guests, but she peeked out the front window just to be sure. She beamed when she saw Zachariah's big black Mercedes Benz parked in her driveway. Taking one last look over her living room to make sure every pillow was in place, she opened the front door. Mary greeted the men as they came in wiping their feet on the welcome mat. She was serious about being a gracious host when she had company. Before they were all the way inside she asked, "How are you two? Have a seat on the couch. Can I get you something to drink?"

Zachariah answered, "I sure would like a glass of that good sweet, iced tea that you make. And bring a glass for Joshua too. I know that he'll love it just as much as I do."

Mary noticed Joshua sigh and stare at his dad. Then he sat back on the couch. He finally looked up at her and said, "I'll just have some water please. Thanks."

After Mary served her guest their drink requests she knocked on April's bedroom door before walking in. April was idly lying there staring up at the ceiling. She sweetly announced, "April you have a couple nice looking gentlemen out here concerned about you. Come on out and say hello."

She watched her grandchild walk past her to the living room dragging her feet. She thought *I sure hope this child doesn't do anything to embarrass me.* April settled down on the empty love seat as far away from everyone else as possible. She sat perfectly still like she was trying to blend in with the furniture and disappear.

Mary, Zachariah, and Joshua tried to get April to open up and explain to them what was troubling her. But she gave one-word answers like okay or yes for every question they asked. After a few minutes of this, her irritated grandmother raised her voice and said, "Child we are trying to help you, but you aren't making this easy."

April mumbled, "That's your problem Grandma. You think you are helping me but you aren't. You don't help me when you make me do more chores around here than anyone else and then make me go to bed early. It doesn't help me when you make me come straight home from school without spending any time with my friends. You definitely don't help me by grounding me so I can't see or talk to my boyfriend." She regained her courage and stared her grandmother in the eye and with an attitude announced, "By the way, he isn't my boyfriend anymore. He dumped me 'cause we never got to see each other."

Mary was angry because her grandchild was disrespecting her in front of their company. She wanted to tell her not to bite the hand that feeds her, but quickly caught herself after remembering April's condition the night before. As calmly as she could she replied, "I think you are too young to be worried about some stupid boy. Getting your education should be the only thing on your mind."

When the teenager rolled her eyes, Joshua jumped in.

He asked, "April, remember when we had our talk in my office about someone you loved wanting to set themselves on fire?"

April parted her lips to say something, but quickly closed her mouth.

Mary was impressed that Joshua seemed to have some influence over her. After a few seconds of silence she asked point blank, "April, why did you take those pills that you found? Was it because your boyfriend broke up with you or because of the problems at school?"

She could see April's eyes slowly filling up with tears. April quietly stared down at the carpet like she was trying to wait the three adults out. She was being stubborn and wasn't going to say another word. So Pastor stretched his arm to rub her hand and coaxed, "Come on April. You can tell us anything. We all love you and are trying to help you."

By now Mary had tears in her eyes too. When April looked up and saw her grandmother's tears, she suddenly spilled her guts. "When my teachers told my mom that they were going to keep me back in the eighth-grade last year, Mama told me she was going to fight it. That she wasn't gonna let them do that to me. But she was nowhere to be found the day of my hearing. So, now I'm in eighth grade again and all my friends are in high school without me. Everybody at Sojourner hates me and thinks I'm stupid, including my teachers."

Zachariah had to reach into his pocket and pull out his monogrammed handkerchief for April. She quickly accepted it and wiped her face. There was no holding back her tears anymore. The adults could hardly understand April anymore because she was sobbing and talking so quickly.

"My daddy is gone. The police came and tore up our apartment looking for him. And I don't know if he's ever coming back. Then my Mama started acting different. She is a crackhead who pawned everything Daddy gave us. She always left me, Junior, and Brooklyn alone. And no one ever came to check on us." April slowly turned to her grandmother. "Not even you Grandma."

"That's not true April. I tried to come see you," Mary interrupted.

Zachariah touched Mary's arm, "Let her talk, Mary." Then he turned to April. "Go ahead and finish."

"Now she is in jail and we had to come move in here. You've got all these stupid rules and chores. I can't go anywhere but school and church." Everyone noticed the big emphasis on the word church. She rubbed her forehead and looked at the two men in the room seemingly realizing that she might have offended them.

"It's alright. We know what you mean. Keep going," Joshua assured her.

"I don't have any privacy. I even gotta sleep with my baby sister."

April paused to catch her breath and wipe the snot from her nose before it ran onto her top lip. She kept her eyes glued to Joshua when she announced, "My grandmother hates me and wishes that I had never been born."

"What?" Mary screamed.

"One day, Mama told me that Grandma warned her not to have me in the first place. She said that I would ruin her life if she did. Maybe she was right." April dropped her head and sobbed. "My brother and sister hate me too. The only person I thought really did like me broke up with me and has a new girlfriend already."

Mary got up and put her arms around April and squeezed her as tight as she could. She cried out, "Your Mama was a teenager when she got pregnant with you. I never should have said that to her. But that was before I saw you come in this world and instantly fell in love with you. Baby, is that why you've been so mean to me?"

April nodded her head.

Mary released her hold on April and looked her straight in the eyes, "I don't hate you baby. I'm hard on you because I love you and I want you to grow up and be responsible. You want to hang out in the streets with your friends, but I know what's out there. Your mom and dad were grown and the street got a hold of them and messed their lives up. Just imagine what it would do to a young pretty girl like you. You need to be in the church with God fearing people that love you. Right now you may not understand what I'm doing for you, but when you get older you will appreciate it."

April exhaled and wiped the tears from her eyes.

"And Brooklyn and Junior may not act like it, but they do love you. Think about it, April, you don't always act like you love them either. But I know you do. I see how you tried to take care of them before I came and got you."

All of the adults in the room joined together and assured April that they loved her and didn't want anything bad to happen to her. They tried to tell her that her teachers at her school were just looking out for her well-being also.

The four of them spent the next hour talking to April about what she could do to stay out of trouble and be happy.

At first she shrugged when Joshua asked her what she liked to do. "I like shopping and watching TV." She looked up to the ceiling and kept thinking. "I like listening to the junior choir sing on Sundays."

Mary smiled. "Oh April has a beautiful voice. She sings around the house all the time."

Joshua said, "That's it then. We will have David put her in the junior choir."

April grinned and looked to her grandmother to see if it was okay.

"That sounds like a good idea. She will have fun and meet some new friends. As soon as she gets off punishment, she has my permission to join under one condition."

April popped her lips.

Mary frowned and said, "I just want you to promise to try and behave here and at school."

"Okay. I'll try."

"You are still on punishment for bullying that girl at school-"

"I know Grandma."

Mary held up her finger to April. "Wait a minute. Let me finish. You are still on punishment, but maybe when you get off a couple of your friends can come over for a sleepover or something. I will even rent you some movies from Blockbuster and order some pizzas."

Mary's eyes lit up as she watched her granddaughter quickly wipe away her tears and the ends of her mouth formed into a smile. She hadn't seen that in a while. April even managed to say, "Thanks Grandma."

16

For the last couple of weeks, April noticed the adults in her life being a little nicer and more patient with her. At home, her grandmother asked her if she needed help with her homework. And she wouldn't let April's brother and sister bang on the bathroom door when she took one of her long baths. At church, Pastor and Joshua gave her big hugs and kisses on her cheek as soon as they saw her. She did have to spend her time at in-school suspension. But after it was over and she got to go back to her normal schedule, even Mrs. Johnson seemed nicer to her. April suspected that her grandmother had something to do with that.

It was almost time for her to finally get off punishment. So she was trying not to give anyone a reason to get mad at her, especially her grandmother. April was looking forward to having a couple girls from school over on the weekend. She hadn't had a sleepover in a long time. At home, she was too afraid of her mom walking in embarrassing her by being high and looking raggedy. When she came home, she was always grouchy. April realized that it was because she couldn't get any more drugs. She didn't have to worry about that anymore because her grandmother always looked nice and was very sweet to company. Her straitlaced grandmother had probably never been drunk or high a day in her life.

During class Friday, April was so anxious about her sleepover that she could hardly sit still or pay attention to any of her teachers. She was too busy watching the clock and imagining all of the fun she and her friends would have that night. Tasha and Quanna became friends because they lived near each other in the projects. Hanging with April made them look cooler and associating with them made April seem smarter.

After school, April anxiously waited for her friends outside the main entrance. By the time they finally emerged, the bus they needed to catch was pulling off. So, the three of them took their time talking and laughing as they walked to April's house. When there was a sidewalk, it wasn't big enough for three people with backpacks and bags to walk side by side. So April gladly walked behind them. She was just happy to have them as company.

The girls got a lot of attention together that afternoon. They were all cute. A small group of men hanging out in front of a convenience store started catcalling as they walked past. There wasn't anything special about the guys other than the fact that they were grown. April followed her friend's lead and waved back at the guys. The girls enjoyed the propositions but never stopped walking. During the four-mile walk, they also got a few horns blown at them. April loved that this was starting out to be a fun weekend.

When they finally stopped laughing about all the guys trying to hit on them, Tasha and Quanna started talking about their boyfriends. April was quiet, anxiously waiting for the subject to change. They had each been dating their boyfriends for a few months. Tasha asked, "You don't mind if I call my boyfriend later do you, April?"

April put a fake smile on her face and answered, "Uh-unh."

Then Quanna quickly chimed in, "Good. Then I'll call mine too. We talk on the phone every night." The two of them giggled and kept walking. April sighed and popped her lips. She wished she still had a boyfriend of her own to giggle about with them.

When they arrived at the house, they said friendly hellos to April's grandmother. April took note of her sweeping off the front porch. That chore belonged to Brooklyn. Clearly her grandmother was wondering where they were so she ventured outside. She was grateful that her grandmother didn't chastise her in front of her company for missing the bus though.

April led her guests to her bedroom so they could put down their bags. Both girls looked around at the room. Tasha, the more vocal one asked, "Why don't you hang up some Bell Biv DeVoe posters or something? I just put up some MC Hammer posters on my walls." April watched Tasha do a quick Hammer move as she sang "*Can't Touch*

This." When she finished she exclaimed, "This looks like an old person's room."

She looked around her room at the plain queen-sized bed with its cherry wood headboard, matching dresser, and nightstand. A yellow lamp that looked like it was older than she was, sat on the nightstand. The dresser was lined with cheap large gold and small silver frames of pictures. Most of them were of baby pictures of April and her siblings. A couple of them were of her mother when she was a baby and then a teenager. April wished that there was a picture of her dad too, but there wasn't. Lastly, there was a generic oil painting of flowers hanging over the bed. Her friend was right. It did look like an old person's room.

All of a sudden the night wasn't turning out how April pictured it. Tasha had managed to say two things already to hurt her feelings. So April snapped, "Well maybe I don't like MC Hammer." She added, "He's ugly anyway," for good measure. The truth was that she had been in trouble with her grandmother practically from day one. Asking to decorate a room in her grandmother's house hadn't even crossed her mind until Tasha mentioned it.

Tasha and Quanna looked at each other and busted out laughing. "Girl, why are you lying? You talk about Hammer all the time."

Quanna stopped laughing and warned, "Y'all don't start arguing. It's too early to come inside anyway. Why don't we go hangout somewhere?"

April regained her enthusiasm. She announced, "My grandmother said that she would take us to Pizza Hut to get a couple pizzas and we can rent some movies. And I'll ask her if we can catch the bus to the mall tomorrow."

This seemed to satisfy the girls momentarily, but it wasn't time to leave yet so boredom quickly set in. Tasha asked, "Where's your CD player? I brought a bunch of CDs for us to listen to." April didn't answer at first. She just took in a deep breath and exhaled. "Don't tell me you don't even have a CD player," Tasha persisted.

April tried to make light of the situation. She answered, "Girl, my grandmother is living in the past. She never bought a CD player. I don't even think she has a tape player. She still has a record player on her shelf." When her company busted out laughing again, April gritted her teeth and stuck up her middle finger.

After a few seconds, which seemed like hours, Quanna tried to save her friend from any more embarrassment. She said, "Don't feel bad 'cause my grandma got that same old stuff in her attic."

Tasha finally stopped laughing and pulled her Walkman and headphone out of her bag to get ready to listen to music herself. Quanna looked at April's dejected face and quickly jumped in again to save her. She dug in her bag and pulled out her portable radio so everyone could listen to music together.

The truth was their dad had bought a nice stereo system, video game systems, big screen televisions, and CD players for his family a long time ago. When he took off, he left them everything except his clothes. But it wasn't long before things started disappearing from home piece by piece.

In the beginning April would ask, "Mom what happened to the CD player that was in your room?"

Her mother would scratch her head and say, "Oh I loaned it to my friend 'cause she is having company."

But when April came home from school one day and a TV was gone, she frantically asked. "Mama, the big screen is gone. What happened?"

Her mother would mumble, "We got robbed."

April didn't know any better so she believed her mother the first two times that she gave her the robbery story. By the third time, April knew that her mother was lying through her teeth. Anyone with any sense would be scared or angry if their apartment kept getting robbed. But her mother showed no real emotion. Every time she said, "We got robbed," her head hung low.

One day April boldly asked, "How do we keep getting robbed in the middle of the day? Were you here when it happened? Did you call the police? Are we gonna move or are we gonna just stay here and let somebody steal everything we own?"

Her mother blew out a cloud of smoke and yelled, "It wasn't your stuff to begin with little girl. You don't own anything. And if I decide that we're gonna move, I'll let you know."

April's eyes squinted. She looked real close at the woman sitting before her at the kitchen table. Felicia didn't look like her mother anymore. Her mother kept her hair done. As a matter of fact, she had a cute new style every two weeks. She also kept her nails looking nice. The polish always seemed to match her outfits.

This woman's hair hadn't had a touch up in months. She usually had it hidden under a baseball cap lately. The stranger in front of her had dirt underneath her nails which was something that her mother wouldn't allow anyone in the family to have, not even Anthony, because she said it was nasty. And when did she start smoking cigarettes?

At first, April thought that her mother was depressed about their dad leaving. Then she thought her mother might be sick. So she sincerely asked, "Mama, are you feeling okay?"

Her mother's eyes were narrow when she looked at her. With contempt in her voice she answered, "I'm fine. Go somewhere and leave me alone," as she put out her cigarette in an ashtray. Suddenly April noticed the similarities. She had seen them on the street corners. And there were the ones that angered her father when they boldly approached him in front of his kids. But she never thought that she would be living in the same apartment with a crackhead.

They taught kids about the dangers of smoking in school. April knew that her mother would eventually kill herself one way or another. So she sat back and patiently waited for it to happen.

Later that night, the three girls talked, laughed, ate pepperoni pizza, and watched two horror movies. Everyone else in the house had gone to bed. Her grandmother had done a wonderful job keeping her little brother and sister away from them. She even made Brooklyn sleep with her in her king size bed which made April extremely happy. So the three teenagers had her bedroom and the living room all to themselves.

After watching the movies, they started playing Dominoes. Tasha kept winning easily, so she suggested that they play Truth or Dare. Puzzled, April and Quanna looked at each. The host asked, "Ain't we a little too old to play that?"

Tasha prodded, "What's the matter, April? Are

you scared to play?" She had a smug look on her face. Neither girl wanted to seem scared, so they reluctantly agreed to play.

When it was April's turn Quanna asked, "Truth or dare?" April didn't want to wake anyone in the house doing a crazy dare so she chose truth. Quanna smiled and asked, "How many times did you and Brandon have sex?"

April was embarrassed but she had to answer. "I dunno, maybe twenty times."

Quanna and Tasha held their mouths wide open and then they started giggling.

By the end of the game, the close friends found out even more about each other. They heard about April and Tasha's sex lives. Quanna was still a virgin, but she had tried pot once. Tasha had almost run out of questions but then she suddenly asked, "You ever tried to kill yourself?"

April hadn't planned on telling anyone about that, but she had to now. "Un-huh. When I caught Brandon at a party with another girl and he started acting like he didn't know me anymore."

Her guests were fascinated with this news. They forgot about the game and bombarded her with more questions. "Why didn't you tell us?"

"I didn't tell anybody. It was a stupid thing to do."

"How'd you do it?"

"I took some pills that I found in the bathroom cabinet."

"And then what happened?"

"My grandmother found me and called an ambulance."

"Does Brandon know?"

"No and he doesn't need to know." April sighed realizing that she had said too much, "Can we talk about something else please?"

It was almost three A.M. by the time the girls turned off the lights and went to bed. And that was only because her grandmother claimed that she couldn't get any sleep because of their chatter. She made them go to bed on one of her many trips to the bathroom which April suspected were opportunities to check on them. Since the bed wasn't big enough for three people, April slept in a sleeping bag on the floor so that her company could have the bed. It was a small price to pay to be able to hang out with her friends.

17

The three girls had such a good time hanging out together at April's house over the weekend. Her grandmother dropped them off at the crowded mall on Saturday where they window shopped, walked around looking at all the cute boys from different schools, and fed their faces in the food court. Then they caught the bus back to her grandmother's house when they were ready to leave. Later on that night, her grandmother took the girls home. But it all changed when they went back to school.

On a trip to the bathroom on Tuesday afternoon, one of her classmates stood next to April at the sinks looking at her weird. April noticed the girl staring at her in the mirror and asked, "Why are you staring at me like that?"

She answered, "I heard that you had a sleepover. That's all."

April felt bad for a second because she realized that the girl might be upset that she hadn't been invited. So she tried to smooth the situation over by saying, "My grandmother only let me have two girls come over otherwise I would've invited you."

Her classmate stopped applying her lipstick and looked at April out the corner of her eye. "Brandon is cute and all, but my mama says that no man is worth dying over."

April abruptly stopped combing her hair. Her left eyebrow went up on its own as she stared at the girl out of the corner of her eye. She snapped, "What are you talking about dying for?"

The younger girl popped her lips and replied, "I heard that when Brandon broke up with you that you tried to kill yourself."

"Who told you that?" April yelled.

At first her classmate shrugged and tried not to answer, but April grabbed her by the shoulders and shook her. Quickly regretting running her mouth, "It was Tasha. She's going around telling everybody," squealed the scared girl.

April let her go and before she knew it her informant scurried out of the bathroom. She stood there in shock. The words hadn't sunken in yet. April had to repeat the words over and over again in her head to make sure that she heard her correctly.

That's why everyone has been looking at me funny today. At first she thought it was just her imagination. Now she knew that it wasn't. She sucked on her bottom lip when a tear came to her eye and she ran in one of the stalls before anyone could walk in and see her sniveling. Inside the bathroom stall her emotion changed from embarrassment to anger. By the time she stormed out of the bathroom she was furious. She marched down the hall headed to Tasha's classroom. April was determined to make her brand-new enemy pay dearly for betraying her.

She barged into the classroom where she knew Tasha was having Earth Science. The teacher was writing on the chalkboard and the students were all sitting down at tables. Everyone jumped a little when the classroom door swung open slamming against the wall behind it.

"I'm looking for Tasha," April announced to the startled instructor. "Where is she?" she hollered impatiently. The students sat quietly at first. Some were gawking at her, others were turning toward Tasha.

The husky boy sitting next to Tasha mumbled, "Wow. This is gonna be a good fight." April looked to see who made that remark and finally noticed her so-called friend.

The teacher moved towards April and tried to grab her arm, but the teen got away from her. "Go get Mr. Brown," the teacher yelled to the student sitting closest to the classroom door. The student hesitated for a second staring at April.

By now everyone including Tasha was on their feet. April was charging towards her bumping into people who weren't smart enough to get out of her way. Tasha had her hands up in front of her and was backing up into the corner. The elderly female Science teacher kept yelling, "Grab her. Somebody grab her by the arm."

One brave skinny boy tried to follow his teacher's instruction, but April swung him across the table like he was a rag doll. The rest of the class was screaming and scrambling to get out of her way when April picked up a metal chair from the table in the middle of the room.

April's nostrils were flaring and she had tears running down her face. "So you wanna talk about me behind my back, huh? You know you're gonna pay for that, right?"

That's when Tasha took off running down a different row headed for the classroom door. April hurled the chair. Several girls started screaming again and everybody ducked. The seat crashed against the wall instead of hitting her intended victim. April's strength was good but her aim was bad. Tasha ran right into Mr. Brown as he was entering the room. They both ducked just in time when they saw April grab another chair and throw it in their direction.

Mr. Brown quickly recovered, ran as fast as he could in his dress shoes, and tackled April to the ground. The principal, teacher, and twenty-five kids looked on in amazement as Mr. Brown, who weighed over two hundred pounds, had trouble trying to control the enraged teen. She hollered, "Let me go. Get off me. I'm gonna kill her!"

The out of breath science teacher asked the principal, "Has this child been referred to the school psychologist? She just came bursting in my room trying to attack one of my students." She threw her hands up and yelled, "Look at my room."

The two women looked around at the room that was in total disarray. One of the tables was knocked over on its side. Two of the chairs were broken, paper and books were scattered across the floor. Most of the students were up on their feet. Some of the girls were crying hysterically while most of the boys were holding their stomachs laughing. The doorway was full of curious students from other classes that came to see what all the commotion was about.

When he finally got April under control, Mr. Brown yelled for the other students to go back to their classrooms. He told the science teacher, "Document everything that you saw and get it to me as soon as possible." He told Tasha that he would send for her later if he needed her. Then he and the principal restrained April and escorted her to the main office.

April was a mess by the time her grandmother arrived at the school. Some of her hair was standing up on top of her head like she had been in a windstorm. The black eyeliner and mascara, that she wasn't supposed to wear, was smeared around her eyes making her look like a raccoon. Her lipstick was smudged across her cheek. She was still so angry that she was rocking back and forth. When she looked up at her grandmother she was glaring down at her shaking her head.

"April, why did you attack that girl? Isn't she the one that was just at our house over the weekend?"

"Cause she had it coming to her. She came back to school telling everybody my business."

"But an eye for an eye makes the whole world blind April. Sometimes you have to turn the other cheek."

April rolled her eyes. "Yeah whatever."

The woman in charge cleared her throat and announced, "Ms. Lewis over the last two years we have referred April to the school nurse, counselor, and social worker."

Her grandmother looked back and forth between her and the principal. "My daughter Felicia didn't tell me about any of this. We were barely speaking until recently."

"The nurse recommended that April get glasses, but I still haven't seen her with any on. Our counselor tried to talk to April about her behavior. She tried to mediate between April and the students that she had problems with. The social worker set up appointments to talk to April's mother, she would say she was coming but it appears that her mother never kept any of the appointments."

April sat quietly with her head down as the two adults exchanged information about her as if she wasn't in the room. Her grandmother interrupted the principal. "Wait a minute. I'm sorry, but I don't know anything about any of that. This is a bit overwhelming."

The principal paused for a moment. "I'm sorry about that Mrs. Lewis. I know that April is embarrassed because she missed so much school last year that we had to retain her. But April's behavior has gotten way out of hand. Not only does she disrupt her own classrooms, but now she is barging in other teacher's classrooms. I can't have her running around my school out of control. If I let her do it, others will think that they can do it too. I'm afraid that April has to be suspended for ten days this time. I'm recommending that she sees a doctor and starts taking whatever medicine that they prescribe her for her behavior."

18

It was choir rehearsal night at Mt. Zion. Zachariah's youngest son David, the minister of music, was in the sanctuary ready to begin. Even though the church was open and full of activity, Zachariah was drained and wanted to go home and relax. On his way out the side door, one of the members of the senior choir stopped him. "Pastor Williams, why are you always running off on choir rehearsal nights? Don't you want to hear us sing?"

Zachariah grinned when he turned and saw who was asking him the questions. She was one of the ladies that was always shamelessly flirting with him. "Well, sister, I do like to get home at a decent hour sometimes. Besides, I like to be surprised on Sunday morning. I don't want to know what songs the choirs are singing until then." He said good night and eased out the door before she thought of a comeback line that would hold him up any longer.

On his way home he stopped at a fast-food restaurant to get a couple of burgers, a large order of fries, and a soda for dinner. When he got home he ate it all within ten minutes and then licked his fingers. Next he cut himself a big piece of the sweet potato pie that one of his female church members baked for him. He got comfortable in his leather recliner to watch sports on ESPN on his fifty-inch big screen TV for the rest of the night.

Zachariah watched a few minutes of the former football star's analyze recent games and try to change their predictions of what teams would make it to the Super Bowl this season. His eyes were starting to get very heavy. Next thing he knew, his head jerked up and a totally different show was on. He reached for his supersized soda and took a big gulp. Just like a little baby, he was trying to fight sleep.

Lately, Zachariah would prefer to sleep down in his recliner rather than climb the stairs to sleep alone in his big empty bed every night. When he first bought this three-story five-bedroom house for his family, he could run up and down the stairs skipping two steps at a time right along with the kids. He remembered his wife yelling at them from the top of the stairs, "Stop running in the house before you break something."

Now that he was in his late fifties, he couldn't skip any of the stairs. And there wasn't anything up there worth straining himself by running. Both boys grew up and moved out years ago. His wife wasn't up there in their master bathroom running his bath water in the Jacuzzi tub like she did faithfully every night until she got sick. Being in this house every night made him realize two things. This was the first time in his life that he had ever lived by himself and that he was tired of being alone.

For the last several weeks, Zachariah had been trying to find the perfect time to ask Mary out on a date. Her husband was gone and now his wife was deceased too. She had been a loyal member of the church since he opened the doors many years ago. He always liked and respected her because she was God fearing and was eager to help anyone that needed it. Lately, his feelings for Mary were more than just respect. Sometimes he was even happy when her granddaughter April acted up so that she would call him for help and he would have an excuse to spend more time with her.

The problem with people like Mary, who are as sweet as they can be to everyone they meet, is that you can't tell if they are as interested in you as you are in them. They are equally nice to everyone. When Mary volunteered and they were alone in his office, he felt special because of the way she smiles at him, talks, and listens to him so attentively. But he noticed when other people were around she was like that with them as well.

So when she baked him a cake or a pie he would always go on and on about how she was a great cook. He was hoping that she would get the hint and invite him over for dinner, but she never did. Mary would just blush and say, "Oh, Pastor, hush. It's nothing really." The next day she would bring him a heaping plate of his favorite foods. What she hadn't figured out was that even though she was a terrific cook, he was more interested in her company than her cooking.

He knew that some people, especially his kids, wouldn't want to see him with anyone else now that his wife was gone. But he wasn't built to spend the rest of his life alone worrying about what everyone else thought about his love life. Before his wife died she told him to go on with his life and be happy.

Sitting alone in his big empty house with the TV watching him and not the other way around, Zachariah decided to turn it off and go sleep in his bed after all. Once he climbed those fourteen stairs, undressed, and slipped into bed, Zachariah wasn't sleepy anymore. He just laid in bed deep in thought.

He decided that he needed to make some changes in his life immediately. The first big change had to do with the church and the other change had to do with Mary. Joshua was about to be thirty, so it was time for him to seriously groom him for his job as future head pastor of the church. The first thing he wanted to do was have Joshua start preaching the sermons every other Sunday so that the congregation could get accustomed to his style of preaching. And Joshua could get used to giving sermons regularly. He would also start shifting other duties off of his desk and on to Joshua's.

Zachariah was proud of the life that he had built. He had started with nothing but a dream and a good woman. With his own blood, sweat, and tears they had turned Mt. Zion into one of Atlanta's best churches. His wife was happy to be married to a hardworking faithful man. Their kids grew up in a good neighborhood and went to great private schools. And he was able to give them everything that they wanted.

Maybe that was the problem with Joshua. He was raised to love the Lord and be responsible, but he seemed to do just enough to get by to reap the benefits. Zachariah felt that Joshua was selfish and spoiled. He enjoyed all the benefits of being a preacher's son but didn't want any of the responsibilities. Zachariah enjoyed getting paid to do what he loved. And he couldn't understand why Joshua didn't feel the same way. What else was Joshua going to do? The only other thing he showed interest in was women. There were too many women as far as Zachariah was concerned.

As far as Mary Lewis, Zachariah decided that he wasn't getting any younger. So he didn't have time to play games. He loved being married. To him having someone to share your dreams with, come home to eat dinner with, a partner to solve your problems with, curl up in bed with every night, and have fun with was the good life that everyone talked about having. Now that his wife was gone, he couldn't think of anyone else in the world that he would want to be with other than Mary. She wasn't a mind reader though. The only way that she would know that he was interested in her and not just being nice, would be to tell her. And that is exactly what he intended to do.

The next day, he called Joshua into his office. "Joshua I've been thinking. I'm not getting any younger. Church business has been putting a strain on me."

"You look fine to me, Dad," Joshua interrupted and then grinned.

"There's no sense in putting it off any longer, son. The church is going to be yours so you might as well have more of a hand in running it now." Zachariah paused for a second when he saw the worried look on his son's face. But then he continued with his thoughts anyway. "I think it is time for you to start preaching on second and fourth Sundays. I would also like you to start going to more of my meetings with me. Eventually, you can preach every Sunday and take care of the meetings and church business without me."

There was suddenly a knock on his office door. “Come in.”

“Hi, Pastor. Are we disturbing you?”

“No, come in. I’ve been expecting you.” Zachariah stood up with a big smile on his face. He moved around to the front of his desk as Joshua stood up too.

“Hi, Joshua. How are you doing?” Mary asked.

“I’m good. I see you brought April with you today.”

Zachariah interrupted, “Yes, I was just getting to that.” He put his arm around Joshua’s shoulder. “April got in some trouble at school. So I told Mary that you could find plenty of work for April to do around here while she is suspended. With your new responsibilities around here, I thought that you would appreciate an extra set of hands to help you out a little bit.”

April looked at Joshua and Joshua looked at April. There was a few seconds of uncomfortable silence so Zachariah squeezed his hand on his son’s shoulder.

Joshua responded by painting a huge fake smile on his face. “Yeah, I’m sure that I can find some work for her to do in my office. Come on, April, let’s get to work.”

Zachariah and Mary peeked out into the hallway and watched April stomped down the hall behind her new temporary boss like a little kid.

"So, you’re back again. You must have missed me," Joshua joked trying to break the ice. “How good are you at answering the phone?"

She declared, "I was born to talk on the phone."

Zachariah and Mary couldn't help but laugh at the suddenly perky teen. "Don't worry. The next two weeks are going to fly by," he said as they stepped back in his office.

19

"Pastor, I honestly don't know how much more of April's behavior my heart can take. The principal said that the school system has been warning Felicia about April's behavior for years. Felicia never told me about any of her problems at school." Mary paced the floor some more and continued her story. "She suggested that April see a doctor to be put on medication because of her behavior."

"I know that the idea of April being on medication is scary to you. But the doctor in the emergency room and the principal both told you that she needs it. If it will help her in school then I think it would be worth it. Did you ask Felicia what she thought?"

She put her head down and was quiet for a minute. Then she sadly answered, "Felicia couldn't do anything for April when she was out on the street because she was busy feeding her addiction. Now, she can't do anything because she's locked up." Mary exhaled. "But to answer your question, she said it's up to me. Of course she used a few more colorful words that I can't use in the house of the Lord. But basically she said that it was my decision to make."

Mary started playing with the cross hanging from her necklace and shaking her head. "I'm not happy about it, but I guess I don't have much of a choice if I want her to continue going to public school. The principal said that the next step would be expulsion. Then she would be placed in the district's alternative school. I don't want that and I don't think a private school would accept her even if I could afford to send her there, which I can't."

Zachariah moved from the big leather chair behind his desk to one of the smaller chairs in front of it. He grabbed Mary's hand and guided her until she was seated next to him. "Mary, all you have to do is ask and I'll do anything that you need me to. I will go to the doctor with you and April or I can go up to the middle school with you or do anything you want me to do to help."

"I like helping you out too. Which is why I spend so much time here at church. But I don't know how much longer I can keep volunteering at Mt. Zion Pastor. Even with all the ladies at the church as customers, Avon isn't enough anymore. I've got three mouths to feed so I'm going to have to find another job."

"I can't lose you Mary. You've been a big help to me. Just keep doing what you're doing and I'll put you on the payroll. I should have done it a long time ago."

"Really? Oh that would be great. Thank you." Mary smiled and said, "And thank you for being so sweet and listening to my problems. I'm sure that you are sick of hearing me complain about my life. You are a man of God and it's not in you to be rude to folks and tell them to be quiet. That's why I'm about to stop bothering you and get to that typing that you need me to do."

She stood up to grab the stack of folders that she was working on the last time she was there. But Zachariah gently grabbed her arm for her to sit back down. He quickly explained, "Mary, you don't understand. I hope that I'm not making you feel uncomfortable, but I'm trying to tell you how much I care about you. You are a sweet, intelligent, beautiful, God fearing woman. And I want to spend a lot more time with you if you're interested."

Mary's heart nearly jumped out of her chest. He wanted her. That was the most romantic thing anyone had ever said to her. Mary covered her face so he wouldn't see her blush. She managed, "Pastor, I don't know what to say." His face went blank. Then his lips grew tight. When he tried to get up from his seat, it was Mary's turn to stop him. She touched his arm and quickly said, "I'm truly flattered. It's been a long time since a man has said those words to me. You just caught me off guard. I'd almost given up hope that you felt this way about me."

"I haven't been spending all of this time with you and wanting you here with me at church just because I'm a man of God. I've been doing it because I want to be with you. But I wasn't sure if you felt the same way."

Mary started laughing. "Well I've seen other female members throwing themselves at you. I would have to be blind not to notice the dresses getting tighter and shorter trying to catch your attention. Of course I have strong feelings for you, but I can't compete with these women."

"Compete? Why do you think I tried to put a stop to all that foolishness when I did a sermon about loose women a couple weeks ago? I noticed all the tension in the congregation when I started preaching." He grinned. "People were looking around at each other. Then the brethren and married sisters finally started clapping their hands, shouting, and shaking their heads in agreement."

Mary smiled too. "Yeah you preached a good one that Sunday. I would imagine that you lost a few admirers that day."

Zachariah turned serious again, "Over the years you've volunteered for just about every job possible here. I remember when you cooked Sunday dinner in the basement kitchen, worked in the credit union, babysat in the nursery so mothers could enjoy church service in peace. You've sold copies of the sermon after service, helped baptize members, and now you serve on the usher board. You could probably do my job too if I let you." He squeezed her hand tight, "Of all people, you should know that I'm not a skirt chaser regardless of whether my wife is gone or not. And I don't care about all these women flirting with me. I know who I want."

That night, Mary couldn't keep herself from smiling. With reassurance from Zachariah, she decided to call the doctor and made an appointment for April. It was time to let go and let God. That included whatever would happen with her love life too. After her husband died, she thought that she would never find love again. But maybe He had other plans for her with Zachariah after all.

Once the kids were in bed, she tried to relax and

watch a little television. Instead, she stared off into space daydreaming. They hadn't set their first official date yet, but Mary was excited about the possibility of a serious relationship with him. What she wasn't looking forward to was the gossiping and envy that she expected once the congregation found out about them being a couple. She knew how women, even church going women, could act if you had something that they wanted.

Mary told herself to slow down. After all, he hadn't explained what "I want to spend more time with you" meant. Maybe it meant something different than what she envisioned. And here she was getting all carried away fantasizing about them like a schoolgirl. Just then the phone rang and Zachariah was on the other end.

"How are you doing Mary? Are you busy?"

"I'm not too busy to talk to you," Mary replied and smiled.

"That's what I want to hear. I'm glad we finally had a chance to have a serious talk about us today. It was long overdue."

Normally, they had quick phone conversations when calling to check on each other. But that night, they talked on the phone for hours and Mary didn't have any doubts anymore that they were on the same page.

20

For the next several days April worked closely with the assistant pastor at the church while her grandmother worked down the hall with the pastor. In the mornings, the four of them had meetings where they discussed what had to be accomplished that day. Then April and Joshua would return to his office. April felt very grown-up working side by side with adults. She loved working alone with Joshua the most.

April thought that working at the church while she was suspended would be a horrible experience. But she was wrong. Joshua made her feel like he was happy to see her every day. Before work she spent extra time in the bathroom getting ready. When she finished, her grandmother sighed and asked, “What are you getting all dolled up for little girl?”

She ignored her question and kept walking.

The extra effort paid off because Joshua gave her a compliment as soon as he saw her. “Well don’t you look nice this morning? You did something different to your hair, didn’t you? It looks good on you.”

“Thank you,” she replied as she tried to hide the smile that was spreading across her face.

Her grandmother would fill up Tupperware containers with leftovers from the dinner that they had cooked together the night before. She brought enough for all of them to have it for lunch in the conference room. April noticed how Pastor went on and on about how good her grandmother’s cooking was. Her grandmother never corrected him to let him know that April put her foot in it too, like the old folks say. She thought it was gross the way those two started being mushy with each other now. When she looked over at Joshua she could tell that he felt the same way. He kept shaking his head and looking in the other direction.

After a few days of this Joshua told April, “I’m going on a food run. What do you want for lunch today? It’s my treat.” The first couple days he brought back fast food. The second week, they had advanced to pizza and Chinese food.

“What do you want from the Chinese restaurant April?”

“I love shrimp fried rice. And can you bring me back some extra fortune cookies, please?” she batted her eyes at him and smiled.

He smiled back and announced, “I’ll see what I can do.”

Thirty minutes later he returned with two orders of

steaming shrimp fried rice and a handful of fortune cookies. April almost screamed when she cracked open her first one and read it. *The man of your dreams is very close by*. She folded it up, slipped it in her pocket, and beamed.

He inquired, “Why are you so happy now? What did it say?”

She just giggled and answered, “Nothing.”

During their meal, Joshua’s direct line rang. April quickly chewed the food in her mouth so that she could sound professional. She enthusiastically said, “Mt. Zion Baptist Church. Joshua William’s office. How can I help you?”

The familiar voice on the other end of the phone politely asked, “Can I speak to Josh please?”

Since he liked to know who was calling him before he got on the phone, April was accustomed to asking. “Can I tell him who's calling?”

The now impatient caller snapped, “This is Tracy, his fiancé.”

April’ face dropped. She tried to hide her disappointment when she announced to Joshua that his fiancé was on the phone for him. She slumped down in her chair and pushed her food away when he thanked her, moved from the small table, and got on the phone at his desk. *This interruption is ruining our lunch.*

“Hey. Can I call you back later?” April scooted back up. *Good. He doesn’t want to talk to her anyway. That’s what she gets for getting smart with me.*

There was a quick pause.

“Oh that was April Lewis. I told you that she’s been helping around here for a few days.” *She’s jealous. Good.*

She should be.

Another short silent break came. April sat quietly wishing she could hear the entire conversation.

"She is Sister Lewis's granddaughter." Joshua listened intently for a minute and then started speaking softer. "I thought we agreed that you would tell all of the wedding vendors that everything was on hold?"

Wow. He doesn't want to marry her anymore. When did that happen? April's eyebrows raised on their own as she strained to listen.

"We'll just have to lose all of our deposits then." He sighed and brought his left hands to his temple and massaged it. "Calm down, okay."

Is she crying? She pulled her plate closer to her and scooped a forkful in her mouth to keep from smiling.

Joshua tried to cut the conversation on the phone short again by telling Tracy, "Look, we'll have to talk about this later. I'm kind of busy right now. I'll see you when I get home."

Do they live together? I didn't know preachers shacked up.

April could swear she heard yelling coming from the other end of the phone as he was putting it back on the hook.

"Is everything okay?" she innocently asked when he came back to the table to finish eating.

"Yes, nothing for you to worry about."

She started shoveling rice in her mouth again trying to keep a straight face.

"It's quitting time," Joshua announced. April frowned when she looked at the clock. "I want to thank you for helping me get my office organized April. I'm used to working by myself, but we made a great team."

She managed to say, "No problem. I actually had fun."

"You did?"

April replied, "Yeah." Now was her chance. April scratched her forehead and asked, "Umm, do you mind if we take a picture?"

She watched him tilt his head and his eyebrows scrunch up. "A picture? For what?"

April shrugged. "I don't know. I always take pictures when I go somewhere or do something. I've been volunteering here for two weeks and haven't taken any pictures."

Joshua chuckled a little. "Okay, I guess that's cool."

He had to lean down to get in the frame of the picture with her. She had a huge smile on her face when she snapped the shot on her disposable camera.

Joshua cleared his throat. "All right. Well I guess I will see you Sunday." When he stepped in front of April and spread his arms open, she didn't hesitate for a second. She walked right up to his chest and wrapped her arms around him. Her face rested against his soft cashmere sweater as she inhaled his masculine cologne. After a couple seconds Joshua gently tried to wiggle loose from the teenager's firm grip. That's when it happened. April felt his pecs flex which made her spread her fingers and squeeze him even harder.

"April?"

"Huh? Oh. Sorry." She quickly dropped her arms down to her side realizing for the first time that he wasn't hugging her back anymore. "Okay. See you Sunday," she said before walking down the hall to meet her grandmother. April left her temporary refuge for the last two weeks with her head hung low. She knew that she would dream about him again like she did last night. Instead of eating takeout food, they were eating a big dinner that she prepared all by herself. She served him his favorite, steak cooked medium well, golden fried shrimp, a loaded baked potato, and a glass of wine. He smiled at her with his sparkling white teeth. After dinner, he gave a long thank you kiss in return. She would fall asleep with a big smile on her face tonight.

21

April had enjoyed volunteering at Mt. Zion so much that she forgot that she had a doctor's appointment coming up. When her grandmother sat her down and reminded her how the doctor at the hospital and her principal recommended she start taking medicine, she whined. "I don't wanna go back to that stupid school anyway. Can't I just transfer to a different school?"

"Baby, we live in school districts. This is the middle school that you have to go to because of where we live. I'm not moving from my home or lying about where you live so that you can change schools. People get in trouble for doing that." Her grandmother looked April straight in her eyes. "Besides, April, your school files follow you everywhere you go. One look at your folder and the next school might demand the same thing. If you can't control your behavior on your own then the medicine will help you." She softened her tone, "This is a good thing baby."

April was pissed off that her grandmother was giving in to the school and making her go to the doctor. Her mother was a crackhead, and maybe even a whore, but at least she didn't drag her to the doctor and force her to take medicine. Everyone in her Math classroom knew what time the ADHD boy in the back of the room needed to go to the office to get his pill. Whenever he started acting weird someone would comment, "Oh shut up and go take your medicine." Everyone else in the classroom, including her, would burst out laughing. Now April realized that the entire classroom may soon be laughing at her too if they found out.

She was downright rude and nasty at the doctor's office. She snapped at her grandmother, "Why didn't you tell me that this doctor was a shrink doctor not a real doctor? You two don't really think that I'm going to lie on a couch and spill my guts, do you?"

Mary looked around the small waiting room to see if anyone was paying attention to them. Then she leaned over in her chair as close to April's ear as she could. "If you think your life is unpleasant now, you don't want to know how awful it will be if you don't answer the psychiatrist's questions. And I mean honestly and without an attitude little girl."

April felt a little drop of spit hit her cheek. She was disgusted and quickly wiped it off. But she knew better than to test her grandmother. She wasn't ready to feel the sting of her grandmother's back hand across her face again.

Between waiting in the lobby, April's private session

with the doctor, Mary's private consultation, and speaking with the doctor together, they were at the medical center for over three hours. In the end, April had two prescriptions. The psychiatrist prescribed Ritalin for April's attention deficit hyperactivity disorder and Prozac for her depression. She explained how these conditions were causing her to act out. They were warned that the medicine may take several weeks to be absorbed in her system and take effect. The doctor also sent them home with an official letter for the school so that April could return to her classes.

The next day, April and her grandmother were in the principal's office bright and early to get April back to her normal routine. Her first day back, April tried to keep her mind off her problems by fantasizing about Joshua. He had been so sweet to her. And unlike the immature boys at her middle school, he was cool without even trying to be. Some days he came to work dressed up in a nice suit because he had meetings. Other days, he came dressed in casual clothes. Either way, he always looked and smelled good. She wished that she was back at the church with him now instead of at her school.

At lunchtime, she ate with her class at their assigned table. As usual, the girls were bragging. They were constantly trying to outdo each other. Today's topic was boyfriends. One of them proudly spoke, "Did you see the jacket that I had on today? My boyfriend let me wear his letterman jacket this week. He's a senior and starts on the football and basketball teams at Grady." One of the other girls popped her lips in disbelief. The girl heard her and defended herself. "I don't care if you don't believe me. When I come to school with pictures of us at his senior prom in a few months you're gonna feel real stupid."

The other girls at the table chimed in and started bragging about their older guys too. April wished they would shut up and let her enjoy pizza day in peace. It was the only cafeteria food that tasted good. One of them stopped boasting and asked, "What about you, April?"

Another girl at the end of the long lunch table interrupted and announced, "April doesn't have a boyfriend. Brandon dumped her, remember?" Everyone listening either chuckled or looked away and tried not to laugh in April's face. April instinct told her to get up and go smack the girl across her face with her heavy lunch tray, but she decided on a different approach.

She smugly stated, "I hate to burst your little bubble, but my man is way better than the boys that all of you have." Everyone at the table was ready for one of April's famous fights. They looked at the girl to see what she was going to say next. She was slow to respond so the crowd turned their attention back to April for her to continue. "He's much older, has already graduated from college and everything. My baby is good looking, has a job, a sports car, a big house, and money"

Someone interrupted, "Yeah right. If he's so great, then why isn't he married?"

"He called his wedding off. Our only problem is his ex-fiancée who won't leave him alone."

"His fiancée?" the girls asked in unison. Now her captive audience shook their heads and stared at April and each other in disbelief.

One of the bolder girls yelled, "Ain't no grown man with all that interested in a girl like you."

April quickly defended herself, “He doesn’t see me as a girl. Anyway, you’re just jealous because you don’t have a man buying you stuff like I do.”

The girl stood up and asked, “Well what’s this big baller’s name then?” April realized that she may have gone too far so she was quiet for a few seconds. The triumphant teen stood up and declared, “See?” She looked around at the other girls at their table for reassurance. Then rolled her neck and stated with confidence, “She doesn't have a man. She’s lying.”

April jumped up too and yelled, “I’m not lying. His name is Joshua Williams if you must know.” She was happy she begged her grandmother to get the pictures in her disposable camera developed already. April whipped the picture out of her and Joshua from her purse and slapped it down on the lunch table like she had just won Dominoes.

22

"All right that's enough. Everybody sit down and be quiet so we can get started." Mrs. Johnson soon realized that most of her students weren't listening though. Except April that is. She was sitting down quietly, which surprised her because April was usually at the center of any commotion.

Mrs. Johnson's students came back from the cafeteria more worked up and excited than usual. She didn't know why. All she knew was that it was taking longer than normal to get them to settle down. Usually, one of the kids would've let her know the big news that had them so excited by now. So she turned and asked, "What's going on?" The question came out like a mother who knew that her children were hiding something.

Her student who saw a speech pathologist twice a week for stuttering yelled out, "April is dating a grown man." His pathologist always encouraged him to speak up more in class. So Mrs. Johnson knew that at that moment, he was proud that he was the one to report the news without stuttering.

April's mouth dropped open and her eyes got very big. She quickly turned to Mrs. Johnson who was staring directly at her. April popped her lips and hollered back at the boy. "Shut up, SPED. Nobody likes a snitch." Then she turned back to Mrs. Johnson. "Don't believe him, Mrs. Johnson. I don't know what he is talking about."

Mrs. Johnson hated when the kids used derogatory words about each other implying that someone needed to be in a special education class. He was actually a very smart kid. If her students hadn't been so busy teasing him about his stuttering, they would realize that. But the fact that April looked scared let her know that there was something more important that she needed to be concerned about at the moment.

Another courageous male student shouted, "That ain't what you said in the cafeteria when you were bragging about that old dude buying you stuff."

April angrily turned towards the second boy who had spoken up and screamed, "You need to shut up too. Don't take it out on me because your mama's on welfare and you can't afford to buy anyone anything."

The class erupted in oohs, covering of mouths, and laughter. There were two things that April was known for. One was her fighting skills and the other was joning. Everyone wanted to be around to listen to her roast her victim but no one wanted to be on the other end of her insults.

Before Mrs. Johnson could fix her mouth to ask another question, the humiliated boy was up on his feet. So April quickly jumped up on her feet too in a fighting stance. Mrs. Johnson firmly ordered, "Sit your behinds down right now. Neither one of you can afford to get in any more trouble."

They reluctantly sat back down giving each other a look that said we will finish this later. The rest of the class let out groans of disappointment because they didn't get to have ringside seats to another one of April's anticipated championship bouts. They missed out on the last fight because it took place in another classroom down the hall.

"I said that's enough. Take out your books and turn to page fifty," she said slamming down her teacher's manual on her desk for emphasis. Finally, the students simmered down.

When class was dismissed, Mrs. Johnson whispered to a straggler as she finally made her way to the front of the room, "Did April mention the name of this older man?"

The girl chuckled. "Uh-huh. She said her sugar daddy's name is Joshua Williams. She showed us a picture of them. He was a nice-looking guy wearing a suit."

"How old did he look to you?"

Shrugging her shoulder the informant replied, "I don't know. About thirty something I guess."

Mrs. Johnson smiled and said, "Thanks sweetie. I knew I could count on you to help me."

That name sounded familiar. She kept repeating it to herself over and over again. *Joshua Williams. Joshua Williams. I know that name from somewhere.* She was halfway home from work, stuck in traffic on Interstate 285 North when it hit her and her mouth dropped. “No. It couldn’t be,” she tried to convince herself. She inched forward in traffic at twenty-five miles per hour for another mile before she decided to turn back around and go see if her suspicion was right. Even though she would have to backtrack for fifteen minutes, adding an extra thirty minutes onto her drive home, she knew that it would be worth it to prove to herself that she had gotten his name wrong.

She passed by that building twice a day five days a week, once on her way to work and again on her way home. It was in between the middle school and the freeway entrance. She had seen that sign’s reflection on her car window as she whizzed past it in a hurry to get to her destination. But the only time it grabbed her attention was when she got caught by the traffic light at the corner.

The entire ride back, Mrs. Johnson braced herself for the fact that her suspicion could very well be true. After all, April had been bold enough to have sex at school. But was he ballsy enough to mess around with a man of God? A man who was twice her age? She couldn’t believe that she would go that far. Then she pulled up to the empty church parking lot and saw his name and his face as big as day. He was standing next to a man that she assumed was his father on a billboard right next to their church. Her heart began to pound in her chest.

The distinguished looking older man in the picture had his arm around the younger man’s shoulder and looked proud. Mrs. Johnson knew that Pastor Zachariah Williams was well known and loved in the city of Atlanta. The younger man on the billboard looked serious and didn’t smile. Joshua Williams didn't look happy, but he didn't look like a child molester either she reasoned. But what did a child molester look like?

She wondered what the worried look on April's face earlier that day meant. *Is she covering for him because she loves him and is foolish enough to think he loves her too? Is she afraid of what he might do to her if he finds out she told anyone about him?*

Mrs. Johnson didn't know what to do or think. But she knew that she had to do something or say something to someone. She tore herself away from staring at the billboard, got back in her car, and slowly drove away from the church parking lot. Before she knew it, she was pulling into her driveway at home. Her car must have driven itself on cruise control. She couldn't remember anything about her silent ride home, because she was so deep in thought.

Over dinner, she talked to her husband about the situation and he agreed that she needed to do something. He said, "A lot of teenage girls look and act older than they really are, but men need to know that they are off limits. Jesus Christ, he's a preacher. There is no telling how many children he was supposed to be a role model for but ended up taking advantage of."

Her husband was angry and she knew it. The fact that this might not be true and could be a big misunderstanding hadn't even crossed his mind. And that scared her. Mrs. Johnson figured that her husband was just like most people who heard a rumor and automatically considered it a fact. She tried to be the rational one. "Listen. I could be totally wrong. There must be at least thirty men named Joshua Williams in Atlanta alone. Plus she is young. Her idea of an older man could be a nineteen-year-old." She paused for a minute to get her thoughts together before continuing to play devil's advocate. "I mean if I report him and I'm wrong I could be responsible for ruining this man's entire life."

Her husband insisted, "Yes, but if you are right, this man could be responsible for ruining April's entire life."

Mrs. Johnson hardly slept a wink that night. She clumsily got ready for work the next morning yawning and rubbing her eyes the entire time. While ironing her dress, she started thinking about April and almost burned a hole in the delicate fabric. As much as she tried not to think about her job on her own time, she had failed to do so in this case. There were definitely other students in her classes that she felt warm and fuzzy feelings toward. But she was also drawn to her biggest troublemaker because she knew that April was problematic for a reason.

The conversation she had with April's grandmother when she called to inform her that she had tried to commit suicide kept her mind occupied. Hearing about April's dad abandoning her, and her mother doing drugs shed light on why April acted the way she did. April showed the kids at school her tough exterior by acting out, but she had a sensitive side that had her resort to trying to attempting suicide. Her grandmother mentioned that their pastors were counseling April. Mrs. Johnson wondered about that the most. *Did April's grandmother trust Joshua freely with her granddaughter? Was he really a part of her life like April bragged or was she just lying to impress kids that didn't even care about her?* If only April could see that most of them were fake friends. There were those that co-signed everything she said because it was safer to be on her good side than her bad side. Followed by the ones who laughed about her antics because they thought she was an outstanding member of the cool kid's club.

Whether April liked it or not, Mrs. Johnson was determined to take a deeper look into April's life and find out what was really going on before she decided what her next move was going to be.

23

"I need to talk to you, April." A few of her curious classmates looked back over their shoulders with raised eyebrows. But most of the kids were just relieved that it wasn't them being detained as they exited the classroom.

April narrowed her eyes to try and look annoyed, but it was just an act. Deep down inside she knew that her nosey teacher wasn't going to leave the situation from the day before alone. She faked being irritated, because it was better to look annoyed than what she really felt. She clenched her teeth together to keep them from chattering. Her heart was beating so fast and loud that she hoped Mrs. Johnson couldn't hear it.

Once the room was completely cleared of students, Mrs. Johnson quickly closed her wooden classroom door.

Her only student left in the room was still standing so she smiled and instructed, “Have a seat so we can talk.” April sat in the first seat closest to the door for a quick escape when the opportunity presented itself. Mrs. Johnson must have read her mind, because he rolled her desk chair directly in front of her and casually sat down.

April gulped and twisted a strand of her hair. The closeness made her uncomfortable so she leaned as far back as she could in the desk that was not her own.

“So April, do you know why I wanted to talk to you?”

April huffed and narrowed her eyes trying her best to still look aggravated. “Uh-unh. All I know is that I’m about to be late for my next class.”

“Don’t worry. I can write you a hall pass. And I have my planning period next, so no one will interrupt us.” She folded her hands on her lap. “I think we need to talk about what happened yesterday.” They were both quiet for a few seconds. “I’m just concerned that you might be doing something that you shouldn’t be doing.”

April stood up and declared, “You don’t have to worry about me. Can I go now?”

Mrs. Johnson smiled, looked up at April and politely said, “Sit back down please.” April slung herself back down so hard that she actually hurt herself. She winched but tried to act unfazed.

“You are wrong, sweetie. I think I have plenty of reasons to worry about you.”

April frowned for real this time and answered, “Mrs. Johnson, I’ve got all the people I can handle worrying about me right now. Besides, all you gotta do is teach me. I don’t think they pay you to be nosey." She turned her head and looked up at the ceiling when she made her last remark.

Her persistent teacher continued. "Listen April, I know that we may have gotten off to a horrible start at the beginning of the school year. But teachers are not just limited to teaching you from a textbook. Believe it or not, I spend all day with my students so it's hard not to care about each of you."

The second bell ringing caused each of them to jump a little.

"I'm actually not that much older than you really. I know you're the oldest and don't have an older sister to talk to. But if you need to, you can always talk to me about anything."

April quickly looked at her teacher. Then she started smiling. Mrs. Johnson smiled back until April started laughing in her face. "How stupid do you think I am?"

"What are you talking about, April?" She asked, not hiding how the insult caught her off guard.

April loudly answered, "One day you hate me and the next day you want to be my big sister. Just stop fronting. Okay?"

Mrs. Johnson hesitated for a few seconds with her elbow on the armrest and her chin resting in her hand. Then she blurted out, "The only Joshua Williams that I know is a minister over at Mt. Zion Baptist Church. Is he the older man that you are dating April?"

April looked back up to the ceiling and tried to remember the conversation in the classroom the day before. She could feel her leg start to shake so she positioned her hand and pushed down hard to make it stop. "They never said that. Who told you his name?"

"So that is his name?"

April tried to keep a Poker face, but on the inside she was cursing herself for saying his name at the lunch table the day before. Her heart hurt because it was beating so hard. All she could do now to save herself was try to convince her meddling teacher not to worry.

She was almost whining when she confessed, "Yes, I was bragging about Joshua Williams. But I swear to God I was lying. They're always talking about their boyfriends and laughing saying that I don't have a boyfriend because nobody wants me. I just lied and started bragging like them. They said I was lying and asked for his name. I spent the last two weeks volunteering at our church with him. So he was the first person that popped in my head." She blew out a deep breath. "I just blurted his name out."

Mrs. Johnson leaned her head back. "Of all the names you could have used, why would you use his name?"

"You don't understand. They were saying that they had older boyfriends in high school. I just wanted to make them feel stupid by saying that my boyfriend was way older than theirs." She was going to try to keep explaining but stopped when she heard her teacher sigh heavily.

"April, did it ever cross your mind that those girls were lying just like you were?"

"No," she honestly answered. "I didn't think about that."

Her teacher scolded, "If I figured out who you were talking about, how do you know that they won't? Don't you realize that you are a minor and he could go to jail?"

"I wasn't trying to get him in trouble." Her voice

cracked and tears started rolling down her face.

Mrs. Johnson stared at her student as they sat silently. "You're not covering for him are you?"

"No. What do you mean?"

"Has he tried to mess with you, April?"

"No, Mrs. Johnson he hasn't." April's leg started jumping again.

Her teacher stared at her intensely. April used the sleeve of her shirt to wipe her face. "He's never touched me. I swear to God I'm telling you the truth. Can I please go now?" she whined.

After her teacher took a deep breath she narrowed her eyes like she was trying to look through her. Finally, Mrs. Johnson seemed to give up. She slowly walked over to her desk and wrote something down. When she turned back towards April she was relieved to see a hall pass in her hand. She extended it to April and answered, "Yes, you can go now."

April snatched the pass and bolted out of the room before she changed her mind. She didn't usually talk to God. But she found herself praying that Mrs. Johnson would find someone else to worry about and leave her alone.

24

The afterschool bus was crowded as usual. A few two-person seats now held three people because girls sat on boys' laps to keep from standing. Other kids stood in the aisle and held on for dear life when the bus turned corners. The cool kids usually congregated in the back of the bus as far away from the bus driver as possible so they could turn on music, light up a joint, and talk about people. It wasn't uncommon for the driver to pull the bus over and threaten to kick people off. Occasionally, they gave him so much trouble that he would get on his radio and ask dispatch to call the police for him.

Usually, April would push through the crowd to be in the thick of what was happening in the rear. But today wasn't a normal day. She was honestly shaken for the first time in a long time. Her mind was occupied wondering about Mrs. Johnson. *What am I gonna do if she calls Grandma and tells her what I did? With my luck, she probably knows Joshua or his fiancée and is going to tell them what happened.*

Every scenario that she contemplated was worse than the one before it. She had to fight to hold back the tears from welling up in her eyes, because she didn't want anyone on the bus to see her crying and start asking questions. As soon as her bus stop came, she made a mad dash to the door and ran up the street to her grandmother's house. This was one of the rare occasions when she was actually happy to be home from school. Her brother and sister were doing homework in the living room. April ran past them but stopped dead in her tracks in front of the closed bathroom door. Before she could turn around and head in the direction of her bedroom, the bathroom door swung open startling her.

"What's wrong with you? What are you so jumpy about?" her concerned grandmother asked.

"Nothing," April lied and said. "It's just cold outside and I need to use the bathroom." She pushed past her grandmother and rudely closed the door in her face. Putting her ear up against the inside of the wooden bathroom door. April kept her ear pressed against the door until she heard footsteps walking away from the door headed towards the kitchen. Then she heard her grandmother talking to her brother and sister in the other room.

When she felt like the coast was finally clear, she flushed the noisy toilet that took forever to fill it's tank back up, ran the faucet full blast and let her tears flow. She regretted every word of the lie she said while boasting to the people at her lunch table. She just wanted to be smarter and more popular than she was. Now she just felt dumb and she was more alone than ever. She would have stayed in her refuge forever if she could, but as usual one of her siblings knocked on the door. "April, stop hogging the bathroom. I've got to use it. And grandma said that you need to hurry up and do your homework so we can eat dinner before choir rehearsal."

April's head jerked toward the bathroom door. With everything that was going on, she had completely forgotten about choir rehearsal tonight. Before today, she had been looking forward to going to practice and being in the junior choir. But now, she didn't want to take the chance of running into Joshua at church tonight.

It was so easy to say his name yesterday. She thought about him all the time now and was still dreaming about him at night too. But she wasn't so naïve to think that he liked her with the same intensity. April reasoned that if there wasn't such a huge age difference between them, she would have a chance to be with him. Just then she remembered that tomorrow was Joshua's birthday. Her spirits were instantly lifted.

April left out of the bathroom, rushed down the hallway to her bedroom, and quietly closed the door behind her. She went to her underwear drawer and picked up her small stash of cash to see what she could afford to buy him as a birthday gift.

If I buy him a nice gift it will make up for what I did and he'll realize how I feel about him. But she knew her grandma wasn't going to let her go to the store before rehearsal. As the teenager sat on the edge of her bed trying to come up with a solution to her problem, she got a sharp pain in her abdomen. Instinctively, she rubbed her stomach and an idea popped in her mind. Jumping off her bed, she snuck back into the bathroom. After removing a small plastic bag, she crept back to her room to hide it in the back of her closet behind some of her grandmother's old shoe boxes. Then she took her homework out of her backpack and hoped that her plan would work.

About thirty minutes later their grandmother called everyone to dinner. The rest of the family was sitting around the table talking to each other about their day. April was still deep in thought about her current situation and Joshua. Her thoughts were interrupted when her grandmother announced, "Let's get going people. It's time for choir rehearsal."

Now was April's only chance to speak up. "Grandma I need to stop at the store first." She braced herself for the series of questions that would follow her announcement.

Her grandmother didn't even stop what she was doing, when she asked, "For what, April? We don't have time for that."

April put on a whining face and almost stuttered as she lied to try to explain, "I think I'm about to start my period and I don't have any pads."

Her grandmother waved her hand like she was shoeing a fly away and declared, "Yes you do. I just put a brand-new pack in there last month. I know they aren't gone already."

"Yes, they are," she quickly disputed.

Her grandmother stopped putting the leftovers in plastic containers and walked right past her oldest grandchild. Headed towards the bathroom, she was on a mission to prove April wrong. And April was right on her heels. She was disappointed when she couldn't find the package under the sink where April usually kept it. Her grandmother practically pulled everything out of the cabinet on her search. The floor was now covered with glass spray, cleansers with or without bleach, cleaning rags, drain cleaner, and toilet paper.

April stared at her from the bathroom doorway and interrupted, "I told you that I used them already, Grandma."

Frustrated, Mary stormed out of the bathroom mumbling something under her breath about no time, not enough money, and too many kids. April smiled because she knew that they were on their way to the store. Now, all she had to do was work out going inside alone. She didn't understand why everyone in the house had to go to church just because she had choir rehearsal. It was useless to complain though. They would all live at the church if it was up to her grandmother.

When they pulled into the drugstore parking lot, April's brother asked, "Grandma can I go get a candy bar?"

April huffed and asked, "Grandma, can you just give me the money and let me go in alone?"

"Anthony, you already had enough candy today." To April's surprise, her grandmother fumbled in her purse and handed her some money. "Hurry up April. I don't want you to be late to your first rehearsal."

She walked nonchalantly to the front door of the store. Once inside she ran to the cologne counter and looked for the one that her dad used to smell good in. When she tried to slide the door open, she realized that the glass case was locked. So April had to hurry and find an employee to unlock it. Then she had to grab some maxi pads and get through the checkout line before her grandmother sent someone in to see what was taking her so long.

The bottle of cologne cleaned her out of the money she had been saving from selling candy at school. But Joshua was worth it, she reasoned. On the walk back to the car, she imagined the pleased look on his face when she gave him his present.

While everyone else in her family was piling out of the car, April was cramming the cologne in her purse. She went to the church restroom under the pretense of using what she purchased at the drugstore. In actuality, she used this time to peel the price tag off. Of course she had to be cute, so she combed her hair again then headed straight to Joshua's office before rehearsal started.

April quickly crept up the stairs and down the hall to the assistant pastor's office. When no one was coming her way, she knocked on his door. She was relieved when she heard him say, "Come in." She stepped in and quietly closed his door behind her. He was in there alone reading through some paperwork.

Joshua looked surprised to see her back in his office. "Hey April, what brings you here?" April smiled because he was smiling. But she was so nervous that she felt her knees shaking.

She slowly walked towards his desk while she got up the nerve to speak. "I remembered that tomorrow is your birthday so I brought you something." That's when she pulled the unwrapped bottle of cologne out of hiding from her purse and placed it on the desk in front of him.

His eyebrows scrunched together and he cleared his throat. He picked it up and stated, "That was very sweet of you and your family to buy me a birthday present. Thank you very much".

In a split second, April's smile melted away. She frowned and replied, "Uh-unh. I bought this by myself. It's a gift from me to you."

He got up from behind his desk and moved closer to her. "April, like I said this is really sweet, but I can't accept this from you. Why don't you wait until it is Pastor's birthday and give it to him? He is the head of the church and the one that deserves a gift not me. Besides, where did you get the money to pay for this?"

April was insulted that he was rejecting her present and treating her like a child on top of that. "I've got money," she snapped. Then she cleared her throat and exhaled to regain her composure realizing that she was acting like a child. "I just wanted to say thank you for being nice to me and to let you know that I remembered that it is your birthday."

Joshua smiled and said, "Thank you April, but I still can't take this gift." He tried to put the cologne back in her hands as he let her down gently.

She stepped back away from the box of cologne as if it were a snake trying to bite her. He said, "You should be able to return it to the store and get your money back."

Knowing that the determined man wasn't going to let up, she reluctantly accepted the box. By the time Joshua turned his back to her, walked back behind his desk, and sat down, April ripped the plastic off, slid the bottle out into her hand, and sprayed his suit before he could object. She proudly declared, "You have to take it now because the store won't let me return an open package."

Joshua coughed and waved his hand in front of his face. She stuffed the exposed bottle back down in the box and placed it back on his desk. "I knew that it would smell good on you. That's why I bought it. I've got to get to choir rehearsal now." She turned and quickly headed towards the exit and called out over her shoulder, "Happy birthday."

A couple of middle-aged female choir members were coming down the hall. They looked at Joshua's office and back at April. They spoke to April with raised eyebrows. "Praise the Lord," they said in unison.

"Praise the Lord," April replied with a big smile. The ladies looked at each other and forced smiles on their faces.

25

Zachariah and Mary had been spending a lot of time together at church. They also talked on the phone every night before they went to bed. When Mary was younger, one of her friends was secretly dating a minister. She remembered her friend justifying why she couldn't tell everyone about them. She explained, "He said that it would be better for us to wait and make sure that we are serious about each other before we let everyone know that we are dating."

Mary thought that his reason sounded suspicious. So she asked her friend, "Are you sleeping together?" Her naïve friend didn't have to say a word because the answer was written all over her face. Without preaching to her friend, Mary just shook her head and looked at her like she was the biggest fool that walked the earth.

Zachariah wasn't like that though. He didn't get up in

front of the congregation and announce that they were dating, but he wasn't hiding it either. Some of the church's daycare teachers were outside with their kids on the playground and saw them holding hands leaving the church together. A few of the deacons knew that they were dating. When they tried to invite him to lunch, Zachariah announced, "Sorry guys. Mary and I already have a lunch date planned." Mary had to put her head down to hide her embarrassment when the deacons curiously looked her way. One of the deacons smiled and patted Zachariah on his back as they walked away.

Today she was going to Joshua's birthday dinner with Zachariah. Mary was so excited about going to the celebration with her new man's family that she went shopping for herself for the first time since the kids moved in. She was so busy buying the kids things to make them comfortable in her home that she had been neglecting her own needs.

It took her awhile to find a pretty blouse that wasn't low cut or too sheer and a pair of new earrings. The salesperson tried to get her to buy a new pair of pants but Mary knew she had pants in her closet that would look nice with her new shirt.

"What about a new pair of shoes?" the energetic sales lady persisted.

Mary knew that the young lady was probably just being nice because she worked on commission. But she hadn't thought about shoes. Looking down at the black leather heels she wore, she observed that the heel was uneven because it was worn down on one side and the back was faded from driving. So she answered, "Only if you have a pair I like that's on sale."

A few minutes later in the shoe department, Mary was just about to give up looking when a nice pair of wedges caught her eye. The salesperson smiled and enthusiastically announced, "Those are fifty percent off."

Mary returned the smile and said, "I'll take them." She felt like a teenager going on a first date.

When she got home from shopping, Brooklyn noticed her shopping bags, jumped up from the couch and asked, "Grandma, what did you buy me?"

Mary laughed and replied, "Nothing for you this time sweetie. I just got a couple things for me to wear tonight. I'm going out to dinner with the pastor and his family to celebrate Joshua's thirtieth birthday."

"If you're going out to dinner, what are we going to eat?" Anthony asked.

"You know I'm not leaving without fixing you something. I'm about to cook your dinner right now."

Brooklyn dug into one of the bags and admired the sparkling earrings that she pulled out. "These are pretty, Grandma." Then she pulled out the heels and slid her tiny feet in them. She took a few steps switching her hips across the living room. Mary smiled. Her brother laughed at her. But April remained quiet.

"Okay that's enough. Put my stuff back in the bag, little girl." She stood there and made sure that Brooklyn did as she was told before she moved. "April, come help me cook."

Mary got the pork chops and onions from the refrigerator and instructed April to get the seasoning, chicken broth, and rice from the cabinet. She smiled at April and stated, "Today, I'm going to show you how to make smothered pork chops and rice."

"Okay," April dryly answered. She was usually happy to help her cook dinner. It was the only time that she was able to bond with her teenage grandchild.

"What's the matter with you?" she asked, folding her arms across her chest.

April pouted and asked, "Why can't we all go to dinner?"

"Tonight is for adults only. You can go another time." Mary turned to wash off and season the pork chops. "Go ahead and start boiling some water for your rice."

April did as instructed and then inquired, "Who else is going to be there? Is Joshua's fiancée going to be there?"

Mary put her hands on her full hips and almost hollered, "Since when do you address adults by their first name like that young lady? His name is Assistant Pastor Williams to you. And what kind of silly question is that anyway? I don't know why Tracy wouldn't be there for her fiancé's birthday dinner."

A couple minutes of silence passed. "Grandma, I'm sure Pastor won't mind me coming with you. You won't even know that I am there and the kids don't need me babysitting them. They're old enough to take care of themselves."

Mary didn't understand her granddaughter's sudden eagerness to tag along with her and Zachariah. Whatever April had on her mind was totally out of the question as far as she was concerned. She sternly answered, "Like I said, this is an adult only dinner. I know that you think that you are grown but you aren't. Do I need to remind you that you are only fifteen years old?" She was about to walk away, but stopped and pointed her finger and warned, "Don't let me find out that you weren't here watching your brother and sister either."

The two remained quiet after their exchange. They only spoke when Mary gave an instruction about what to do next or April had a cooking question. Even though she couldn't wait to go out on her date, deep down Mary felt guilty about leaving the kids at home. She thought about all the nights that she stayed in the house alone wishing that she had a male friend to spend time with. Now she finally had one, but she also had a house full of kids that needed her. Tonight would be the first night in the last couple of months that she would be leaving the house without three shadows trailing behind her.

While slowly stirring the rice, Mary admired the dinner that April and she prepared together. *This looks almost good enough for me to stay home and eat it too.* She smiled to herself when she realized that she was in her comfy kitchen stalling because she was nervous about her first dinner with Zachariah's family as his date. *It's time for you to put your big girl panties on and deal with it.*

Zachariah picked her up right on time just like Mary knew that he would. They were from the old school where it was expected that a gentleman would come inside with flowers in hand and wait with his date's family for the lady to make her grand entrance. Mary shook her head at how so many women accepted their dates honking the horn and sitting outside until the woman came out.

When she walked into the living room wearing her new blouse, earrings, and heels, Zachariah stood up and smoothed out his suit. She admired the new tie and matching pocket square that she'd never seen him wear before and smiled to herself. *He went out and bought something new too.*

Zachariah handed her a bouquet of beautiful red roses. It had been a long time since a handsome man gave her flowers. And Mary couldn't stop the big goofy smile that spread across her face when she saw them.

Her youngest grandchild giggled, then extended her hand and offered, "Can I put your flowers in a vase for you Grandma?"

Once Mary passed her flowers off, Zachariah commented, "You look very pretty tonight Mary."

"Thank you. You're looking pretty good yourself."

Anthony chimed in, "She bought new clothes and everything."

Mary quickly started giving instructions before he told her date any more information. "All right you two April is in charge, so listen to her. Everyone go to bed at your regular bedtimes. Start taking your baths soon. And don't open the door for anyone."

Zachariah lightly touched her shoulder. She acknowledged his concern by moving closer to the front door before saying goodbye to the kids. Mary knew that he didn't want to be late. The two of them ended up being the first ones to arrive at the private dining room at Bone's Restaurant in Buckhead. Two by two, like the animals being boarded on the arc, all of the other couples began to arrive. First David and his wife arrived. Then Joshua's best friend and his wife came. And finally, Joshua and Tracy arrived. It was his celebration but he didn't look happy. Mary wanted to believe otherwise, but she could tell that it was because of her presence.

At first everyone kind of looked surprised that Zachariah wasn't alone. They made comments like, "Oh. Hi, Mary."

"I didn't know you were going to be here tonight."

"We're happy you could join us."

Tonight was the only time they had ever seen Pastor Williams on a date with anyone. After a few minutes of awkward silence and then boring small talk, Zachariah cracked a joke and everyone laughed and loosened up a bit.

After dinner, everyone else left, but Zachariah and Mary stayed behind. He ordered decaf coffee for them. When their server walked away, Zachariah asked, "So did you have a good time tonight?"

Mary smiled and replied, "I'm still having a good time." She noticed everyone seemed a little uncomfortable at first. So Mary cautiously asked, "Do you think that your sons minded me being here?"

"They've never seen me with anyone other than their mother. I guess it will take a little getting used to. But they know that you are a good woman just like she was. So I'm sure they won't have a problem with it." With that he placed his hand on top of hers to reassure her and smiled.

"How do you think your family feels about you dating me?" he asked in return.

Mary grinned, "You know that the kids love and respect you. You saw the way they were all crowded around you at the house tonight." She immediately thought about Felicia and got quiet.

"What's wrong? You aren't smiling anymore."

His date reluctantly confessed, “I don’t want to ruin our evening. But I was just thinking about Felicia. Being around your family on Joshua’s birthday made me remember that Felicia’s birthday is coming up soon. Not to mention that Thanksgiving is next week. My baby shouldn’t be in jail away from her kids during the holidays.”

“Well how much is her bail?”

“Oh I can’t afford to pay it unless I put my house up for collateral,” she quickly replied.

“Well maybe you can’t afford it, but I’m sure I can pay the percentage that a bail bondsman would need to get her out for you,” he clarified.

Mary waved her hand back and forth. “Oh no. That’s still a few thousand dollars. I can’t ask you to do that.”

Zachariah beamed, squeezed her hand, and explained, “You’re not asking. I’m offering. Just let me know what to do and I’ll take care of it for you.”

Mary opened her mouth to try and turn down his offer again, so he stopped her by covering her mouth with his lips. Initially she tried to pull away, but she quickly reciprocated. After their long passionate kiss, Mary blushed and looked around the restaurant to see if anyone was staring at them. But no one was paying them any attention. She took her napkin and gently wiped her lipstick off of Zachariah’s lips. “I guess I can’t argue with that.”

When she got home from her wonderful date, they noticed the light from the living room TV go out when they pulled in the driveway. She was too happy at the moment to even be angry. “These kids think that they are so slick. I bet when I go in there, they will all be fake snoring like they have been asleep for hours.” They both had a good laugh about that.

Zachariah walked her to the front door, like the gentleman that he was. They gave each other a long goodnight kiss. Before he turned to go, he reminded her, "Don't forget what we talked about. I meant every word I said."

"I really appreciate that, baby. I'll check into that first thing tomorrow and give you a call. Good night."

Mary went to bed that night feeling so good. She always knew that Zachariah was a good man and helped plenty of people when they were in trouble. He made regular visits to hospitals and people's homes when they were sick. She knew about him buying plane tickets when one of the deacons needed to get to his mother's deathbed clear across the country in a hurry. Pastor even helped out when a member lost their job and got behind on rent. But it never crossed her mind to ask him for that much money for her family. Now that things were looking up, she promised herself that when Felicia got out of jail, she would make sure that she stayed off drugs and started being more responsible with her children. This time, Mary would be deeply involved in their lives. There were not going to be any more secrets in her family.

26

When April woke up Thursday morning, her grandmother was walking around the house singing. She strained to hear her and softly sang along when she recognized the words to the old gospel song. April could only assume that they had a really good time on their date at Joshua's birthday dinner. That must be why she was so happy this early in the morning. Her grandmother always sang when she was in a good mood. She got a chill through her body and shook her head in disgust at the thought of her elderly grandmother and the pastor fooling around at their age.

Her grandmother wasn't yelling for anyone to wake up and get to school on time like she usually did. She was calmly telling Anthony and Brooklyn, "Let's get a move on. You don't want to be late for school. I've got some hot oatmeal, sausage, and toast ready for you in the kitchen."

Without seeing her, April could tell that she wore a smile by her cheerful tone.

April was about to get up and ask her grandmother all about the dinner. But then she walked in her bedroom grinning from ear to ear. She sat down on the edge of the bed and whispered, "Pastor Williams said that he would give me the money that I need to bail your mother out of jail."

She sat straight up in her bed and stared at her grandmother. Trying to figure out if she had heard her correctly. She wondered if she was supposed to be happy about another adult squeezed into her grandmother's tiny house trying to tell her what to do?

Her grandmother looked puzzled and asked, "Baby, did you hear what I said?"

April stared at her grandmother and dryly answered, "I heard you."

Mary pulled her head back and narrowed her eyes at April. She shook her head and turned around to leave. But not before she hollered, "Get up out the bed, April. It's time to eat so you can take your medicine and go to school."

April reluctantly dragged herself out of bed and started getting ready. The shocking news that her mother was getting out of jail made her lose her train of thought about Joshua. Wondering what it would be like when her mom got out now occupied her mind. It bothered her all day long in her classes. She hardly heard a word that any of her teachers said. April was grateful that at least Ms. Johnson wasn't bothering her anymore. At the end of school, April wasn't in any hurry to get home, because she wasn't sure if her mother would already be there.

When the school bus rode past Mt. Zion, April

noticed the silver Porsche with the MWLLMS personalized license plate in the parking lot. She knew it was Joshua's car, and when the bus stopped at the red light, April jumped up on a whim and ran off the bus behind a group of kids. Returning to school meant that she didn't get to work in his office and admire his tall, muscular frame every day anymore. She loved staring at his caramel skin when he wasn't paying attention. And he always smelled good too. April wanted to sneak up on him and see if he was wearing the new cologne that she just bought him.

She was grateful that the Pastor's door was closed when she walked by his office. But she stopped walking when she heard a woman talking in Joshua's office.

"Well what am I supposed to think, Josh? You're not answering my calls when I call and you don't have the decency to call me back. You disappear a couple nights a week. Then you come in smelling funny and jump right in the shower."

Joshua calmly replied, "It's not what you think, Tracy."

"And every time I call here some female answers. If it's a kid like you say, then why isn't she in school?"

"I told you. She was suspended from school for two weeks. Her grandmother brought her here when she came to volunteer. Do you think I wanted her here? That girl has some serious issues. But I guess I can't blame her since her daddy was a drug dealer who ran off and left them. Her mama is a filthy crackhead who was running the streets getting high before she went to jail. I mean, I kind of felt sorry for the girl. And my dad was trying to impress her grandmother, so I guess you could say that I was stuck babysitting her for the last two weeks."

April's head jerked back and hit the wall behind her. She wanted to barge in Joshua's office and confront him but her body wouldn't cooperate.

"You know people are talking, right?"

"What people, Tracy? What are you imagining now?"

The woman's voice got even louder and she explained, "That girl is going around telling everybody that you are her boyfriend. My friend's daughter says it's all the kids are talking about at her school."

April could hear Joshua exhale all the way in the hallway.

"Is that what your erratic behavior is all about? The nonstop phone calls and coming up here checking up on me because of a ridiculous rumor?"

"Is it just a rumor, Josh? She said that she saw pictures of you two together."

"What are you talking about? Look, this has got to stop. I know I postponed the wedding when my mother passed away, but maybe we need to call it off entirely."

April heard something break in his office. Then Tracy's voice went up an octave as she asked. "What did you just say to me?"

"I've got a lot of stuff going on right now and I don't need you stressing me out." His voice was getting further away like her was pacing the floor.

Tracy screamed, "Are you serious? You're calling off our wedding because I want to know what was going on with you and that girl?"

"No. I'm calling it off because we were fine before.

Getting engaged messed everything up between us. I was trying to please you. And I was trying to please my mother. But now it's time that I start worrying about myself."

"We were fine before in your eyes, because you were seeing other women. Is that what this is about? You want to see other women, starting with this teenager?"

Joshua's voice got as loud as his fiancé's when he yelled, "You are delusional. Regardless of what I say, you think you've got it all figured out. So I'm done talking." Everything was quiet for a minute. April figured that Tracy was either in shock or waiting for Joshua to change his mind. Finally he said, "I'm sorry but I've got somewhere that I need to be."

"Oh you're sorry alright. But not as sorry as you are going to be!" Tracy hollered as she stormed out of his office with her heels clicking in the opposite direction. April crept back down the hallway, ran down the steps, and out the front door back into the cold November air. She didn't stop running until she was out of breath and in tears.

So he thinks I have serious issues, huh? And he feels sorry for me? He was just babysitting me, huh?

When April got home, she spent a minute wiping her tear-stained face with a mitten that she found in her jacket pocket before she stomped in the house. As soon as she walked in the door Brooklyn and Anthony simultaneously said, "Grandma's been waiting on you."

Their grandmother stepped into the living room and asked, "April, where have you been? I saw the rest of the kids that ride your bus walking down the street ten minutes ago."

April lied and explained, "I missed the bus so I had

to walk home. What's wrong?" She hoped that her grandmother wouldn't stop and do the math. There was no way April could have missed the bus and walked home that fast.

But her grandmother happily replied, "I got the money from Pastor to bail your mother out of jail. The woman behind the window that took the money said that it would take a while to process her for release. I sat down there all morning waiting for your mama. Now that all of you are home safely, I'm going back and see if they let her out yet. I don't want her getting out and not have someone there waiting on her."

Brooklyn was so excited about seeing her mother. She jumped in front of her grandmother and asked, "Grandma, can I go with you to get mommy? I'll be good."

"No baby, you can't go. I don't want you anywhere near that jail. I want all of you to get started on your homework." Then she turned to April, who hadn't said a word. "The meatloaf is in the oven. Take it out in thirty minutes. Everything else is already finished on the stove. I'll be back soon, I hope." Then she hurried out the front door.

As soon as their grandmother pulled out the driveway, April's younger brother disregarded his grandmother's instruction to do their homework and turned the TV on to music videos. April's little sister shook her head, pulled her books out her book bag, and yelled, "Ooooooh. You heard what Grandma said."

Anthony replied, "Shut up and mind your own business." In the meantime, April was already heading towards her bedroom for some privacy. Listening to her younger sibling's meaningless argument was giving her a headache. But slamming the door behind her brought silence to the racket in the living room.

Still sulking on her bed forty-five minutes later, Brooklyn barged in their room. She popped her lips and stared at April who was stretched out across their bed. "Didn't you forget something?"

April didn't feel like being bothered with her know-it-all sister pestering her about some stupid homework. She warned, "If you don't leave me alone little girl, I'm going to break your skinny little neck."

Brooklyn tooted her lips, folded her arms across her eight-year-old chest, and matter-of-factly announced, "Well when the meatloaf burns, the kitchen catches on fire, and the house burns down it will be all your fault."

Suddenly remembering about the meatloaf in the oven, April almost knocked Brooklyn down as she darted past her to open the oven. She yelled over her shoulder, "How long has it been since Grandma left?"

Her little sister, who everyone else thought was so sweet and innocent, was silent as she watched her pull the dry meatloaf out the oven. She hollered, "You mean you are smart enough to be on the honor roll, but you can't turn off an oven?"

"Grandma told you to watch the meatloaf not me, remember?" was her sassy reply. The two of them just stared at each other with animosity for a few seconds until the youngest one came to her senses and blinked. "I saw Grandma putting ketchup on top. Maybe it'd help if you put some more on it."

When April squinted and took a step in her direction, Brooklyn took off running, retreated to the bathroom, and locked the door. April grinned. Her little sister still needed to be reminded from time to time who was the boss. Then she quickly pulled the plastic squeeze bottle of ketchup from the refrigerator and followed her annoying sister's suggestion. The meatloaf didn't look that bad she reasoned. But she wasn't hungry. She had to figure out how to pay Joshua back for breaking her heart. She was determined not to keep letting people use her and throw her away like she was trash.

27

"I'm so glad that you can finally leave this hell hole. Your kids can't wait to see you," Mary told Felicia as she hugged her tightly.

Felicia hugged her mother back and smiled. But she abruptly released her and started walking so quickly to the exit that Mary had to struggle to keep up. Felicia said, "Thank you so much for changing your mind and bailing me out of jail, Ma."

"Oh don't thank me. Zachariah was sweet enough to give me the money to bail your behind out. I want you to go personally thank him."

Felicia stopped dead in her tracks. "Who?"

"Zachariah. I mean Pastor Williams. He gave me the money to bail you out. I told you that we have been seeing each other. We were talking and I told him that I hated for you to be in jail for your birthday and the holidays, so he gave me the money to bail you out."

"Wow. I guess I owe him a big thank you the next time I see him."

Mary smiled, "That'll be on Sunday. I think it's about time that you came back to church. Don't you think so?"

Felicia sighed, "Oh I should have known this came with strings attached."

Mary got in the car and slammed the door. The entire car shook. She gripped the steering wheel to try and calm down but she was about to give Felicia a piece of her mind. This was supposed to be a happy moment. "What is your problem? I would think your time in jail would've made you realize some things. Your life has gone downhill ever since you stopped going to church." She paused and turned to look at her daughter who was rolling her eyes. "Maybe next time I will leave your ungrateful behind to rot in jail."

Felicia flatly stated, "Don't worry, there won't be a next time." She changed Mary's radio station from gospel to R&B without even bothering to ask as they rode home without talking to each other anymore. Mary noticed her daughter rubbing her arms so she turned the heat all the way up. She had on a short sleeve t-shirt even though it was only forty-five degrees. Mary wished that she remembered that it was still warm outside when she got arrested. She would have taken her a warm jacket to wear home.

It was around eight o'clock by the time Mary drove her old car up the driveway. As soon as they saw the beams from the headlights shining through the front window,

Anthony and Brooklyn ran out the door onto the front porch to greet their mother. They hadn't seen her in nearly four months because Mary wouldn't allow them to visit her.

As Mary got out of the car, she could see that April was upset that they had left the front door wide open and were letting the cold air in the house. She mimicked Mary's words when she stomped to the door and yelled, "Were y'all raised in a barn?"

"Come on y'all. Let's get out of the cold," Felicia said.

April tried not to pay her family any attention until Mary gritted her teeth and asked, "April, aren't you going to speak to your mother?"

"Hi," she said without turning and looking at her mother. Mary smiled as she watched her other two grandkids were excited to see their mom.

April finally faced her mother and commented, "I see you got someone to French braid your hair for you."

Mary could tell that April was being a smart aleck. From the weight gain to her new hairstyle, she also noticed the drastic changes in Felicia in the short time that she was away. *It was a shame that she had to go to jail to fix herself up.*

Rubbing the top of her head, "Yeah, a friend of mine did it for me," Felicia said with a smile. She sat down on the couch and attempted to hug her eldest. But April didn't return the embrace until she looked over her mother's shoulder and noticed her grandmother glaring at her with narrow eyes. She exhaled and raised her arms reluctantly patting her mother on the back in place of a loving hug.
Felicia released her and asked, "So baby, how have you been

doing in school?"

April rolled her eyes.

Mary tried to change the mood. She questioned, "Did everyone eat dinner?"

Anthony quickly answered, "Yeah, but the girls burned your meatloaf."

Felicia looked at her only boy and curiously asked, "What do you mean, the girls burned the meatloaf? What's wrong with your hands? I know that I'm not raising a male chauvinist pig. Am I?"

He frowned and asked, "What's a male chauvinist pig?"

Mary and Felicia turned to each other and had a good time laughing. Mary asked, "Are you hungry, Felicia?"

Felicia's eyes lit up like a kid in a candy store. "Yes ma'am I am. And even burnt meatloaf gotta be better than the crap they served us every day," she said as she headed for the kitchen followed by her two young shadows.

Mary, who had gotten used to being in the role of mother to her grandchildren, let the kids stay up past their bedtime to celebrate having their mother back. She hoped that having to catch up on her kid's day to day life would scare Felicia into realizing that her children were going to grow up and she would continue to miss it all if she didn't get her life together.

Finally, Mary announced, "All right kids, it's late. It's time for y'all to get in the bed now."

Brooklyn swung her little head around. She whined, "Grandma, why can't we stay up and talk to Mommy? I didn't get a chance to tell her about the project that I'm making for the Science fair yet."

"I'm sorry, baby. It's getting very late."

Brooklyn broke down and started crying hysterically. Mary tried to calm her down, but she was inconsolable and didn't want to hear anything she had to say. Felicia finally stepped in and gently turned her daughter's tearstained face towards her. She softly said, "Baby, you can tell me all about it tomorrow. It is way past your bedtime and you have to get up in the morning and go to school." Felicia smiled and tried to make her baby smile again. "If you are in bed in the next sixty seconds, I'll come tuck you in."

Her youngest wiped her tears and yelled, "Good night," to whoever was listening and took off running towards the bathroom.

Mary and April looked at each other and shook their heads. He had been glued to his mother's every word all night but Anthony stood up and nonchalantly said, "Good night Ma."

Felicia sighed and demanded, "Boy you'd better get over here and give me a hug."

Mary chuckled as she watched their extra-long hug as his macho man attitude quickly melted away. She tried to sound stern by commanding, "Go put your pajamas on now Anthony." He gave his mother a peck on the cheek and strolled down the hall. Then Mary walked down the hallway too leaving April and Felicia alone.

28

April wasn't impressed with all this family togetherness crap. She knew that Brooklyn wasn't old enough to understand what was going on with their mother before she went to jail. Her brother should understand. But he was too preoccupied playing the one video game that their mother hadn't pawned to realize that his family was falling apart right in front of his face.

She could care less if her mother was around or not. April kind of felt sorry for her because she figured that her problems with the law were not over with. And it was only a matter of time before she was hanging out in the street with her friends getting high again. The teen just wanted everyone to be quiet so she could watch the last few minutes of her new favorite show *The Fresh Prince of Bel Air*. Once she saw the credits come on the screen, April got up to leave the room. She was already tired of looking at the woman she had been stuck with as a mother.

"You've been really quiet tonight."

April just shrugged. She tried to walk away and go to her room. But her mother insisted, "Sit down for a minute. We need to talk."

Just because I'm being forced to sit down, doesn't mean you can make me talk. So she sat down but turned her attention back to the TV. When Felicia picked up the remote and turned the TV off, April slowly turned and gave her mother a cold stare.

If she wants a big smile, hug, and a kiss, she is looking at the wrong child. April shook her head in disgust at her mother. "You really didn't expect me to run to you with open arms like everyone else, did you?"

Felicia snapped, "No. What I expect is a little respect. You'd better watch the way you talk to me young lady. I'm still your mother."

April rolled her eyes up to the ceiling and mumbled under her breath, "Whether I like it or not."

"Keep trying my patience little girl and you'll be sorry you did."

"In case you haven't noticed, I'm not a little girl anymore," April whispered.

Felicia's eyes narrowed when she said, "Okay. Since you're so grown and have so much to say then say it loud enough so I can hear you instead of mumbling. Put your big girl panties on and say it."

"First of all, why should I respect you? We were home alone the last time for almost a week before I found out that you were even in jail. Did you forget about us or something?" April watched her mother turn her head like she couldn't face her anymore. "And who do you think took care of Anthony and Brooklyn all those times that you disappeared?" Pounding her finger into her own chest April shouted, "I did. That's who."

"Humph." Her mother shook her head and laughed. "Just 'cause you fixed a few sandwiches or bowls of noodles for your brother and sister, don't make you grown, April."

She is sitting there looking silly in a t-shirt and shorts, as cold as it is outside, but she has the nerve to laugh at me? Suddenly April wasn't in such a hurry to get away from her mother. She wanted to hurt her. "I'm grown enough to have a man. Where is your man?" But April regretted the words as soon as they left her mouth. When her mother's head jerked back in her direction, it was her turn to quickly look away. April saw her mother's backhand coming her way from the corner of her eye, but she couldn't get out of its way fast enough. Before April could get herself together, her mother was up off the couch hovering over her.

"What man?"

April was too startled to answer. But her mother kept repeating herself. "Don't get scared now. What's his name, April?"

Tears started welling up in her eyes. Reluctantly April stuttered, "Joshua Williams."

"Joshua Williams. Joshua Williams." Felicia kept saying the name out loud like she was trying to figure out where she knew that familiar name from. "Where do you know him from?"

April exhaled. "From Grandma's church."

"What?" she hollered. "You mean the pastor's son?

You mean that Joshua Williams? Felicia plopped down on the couch. "You're kidding, right?"

April knew that it was too late to turn back. She shook her head no but wouldn't speak or look at her mother now. Joshua had hurt her feelings and made her angry, but maybe she should have made up a fake name to get her mother off her back. Her knee started shaking uncontrollably and she wanted to run to her only refuge, the bathroom.

Felicia scolded her daughter and demanded, "April, look at me." She sat back down, placed her hand on April's knee to help her calm down, and covered her face with the palms of her other hand. "Have you been having sex with him?"

April's mouth dropped open. She didn't know how to respond. So finally stuttered, "Um, no. He just touched me a couple times, that's all."

"Touched you where, April?"

April quickly answered, "In his office."

Her mother huffed, "No, I mean what part of your body did he touch?"

April was afraid that her grandmother would hear them because her mother was talking so loud. She looked behind them to see if her grandmother was coming. April frowned and looked at her mother like she was uncomfortable answering. "Right here," she said as she touched her chest.

The two of them were quiet for the next few minutes. April wasn't sure what her mother was thinking. And this wasn't turning out the way that she had expected it to. The subject of sex hadn't crossed her mind.

"Did you say that he was your boyfriend?"

"Uh-huh. We talk a lot. And he buys me lunch all the time. He even came here to see me once."

"He has been here before?"

"Yeah."

Felicia was quiet for a few seconds. Now it was her turn to look down the hall behind them. "Does anyone else know about this?

Her daughter explained, "Well, the kids in my class told my nosey teacher Mrs. Johnson about us. She asked me about it, but I denied it."

"Does your grandmother know about this?" April shook her head no. Felicia looked at her daughter in the eyes and told her, "I need to figure out what to do about this. In the meantime, you stay away from him. Do you understand me?"

April nodded and got up to head to her bedroom. When she slid in the bed, she was surprised that her little sister was fast asleep instead of patiently waiting for their mom to tuck her in like she said. But then again, all of them were used to their mother not keeping her promises by now.

29

"Dad, I need you to come to my office right away."

As soon as his father stepped into the room Joshua ordered, "Close the door, Dad." He tried not to be disrespectful to his father, but his anger showed in his voice and on his face.

His father ignored his rudeness and took a seat next to a familiar looking woman. "Good morning, ummm," he snapped his finger struggling to recall her name.

"Dad, I can tell that you are confused. I didn't recognize her right away either. Then she reminded me who she was."

Their visitor wiggled in her seat uncomfortably as Zachariah stared at her trying to figure out who she was. He quickly gave up and admitted, "Son, I'm afraid I'm getting old so my memory is failing me right now. Why don't you give an old man a break and refresh my memory?"

"Her name is Felicia Lewis. She is Mary's daughter."

Joshua added emphasis on each word when he continued, "The one you just spent all that money on bailing out of jail."

Zachariah narrowed his eyes at him. His nostrils flared and Josh could tell that he wanted to explode. If Joshua wasn't so angry himself, he would have been nervous. His father looked him directly in the eyes and stated, "Son, I knew who she was the second you said Felicia Lewis. You didn't have to embarrass Felicia by reminding her of what happened."

Joshua stared back at his father and answered, "Actually Dad, I think that I do need to remind her of what you just did for her." He could tell by his father's cheeks moving that he was grinding his teeth. Joshua expected his dad to admonish him some more for being extremely disrespectful to Mary's daughter. But he must have figured out that there was more going on in that room than he realized.

He watched his father look away and study Felicia closely. Her hair was braided straight back close to her scalp. She had on a jacket that was too big for her like she had borrowed one of Mary's jackets. It looked like she couldn't weigh more than one hundred pounds now. Her jaws had sunken in and she didn't have on any makeup. The Felicia sitting in his office was not the pretty face, nice body Felicia that they remembered from years ago. She looked like she had been leading a rough life since her absence from church.

His father broke the uncomfortable silence and asked, "Would someone like to tell me what's going on here?"

"Dad -"

Felicia cut Joshua off as he opened his mouth to speak. "Pastor, thanks for giving my Mama the money to get me out of jail. I really appreciate it. But when I got home, I found out some disturbing news."

Zachariah looked back and forth from Mary's daughter to his son. Joshua was shaking his head and looked disgusted. He turned back to Felicia and asked, "What disturbing news did you find out?"

"I found out that my impressionable teenage daughter, April, is being taken advantage of by your son." She turned to Joshua and returned his look of disgust. Felicia continued, "April considers him her boyfriend."

Joshua jumped in by laughing at her statement. He turned to his dad and asked, "Do you believe this Dad? She comes in here accuses me of messing around with a teenage girl and then she asks me for money to keep quiet about it. She threatened to go to the police if I don't give her five thousand dollars."

Zachariah held up his hands for both of them to be quiet. He rubbed his forehead and was quiet for a second. Then he turned to Felicia and asked, "What do you mean by she considers him her boyfriend?"

"She says that he buys her lunch, comes to the house to see her, and that he touches her, if you know what I mean."

Joshua hollered, "Jesus Christ. Stop saying that!" It was the second time in ten minutes that he had heard this crazy story but it still blew him away.

She continued, "Apparently, her teacher and the kids at her school know about it too." Zachariah quickly turned to his son with a surprised questioning look on his face. So Felicia snidely remarked, "I guess you didn't know about that either."

The assistant pastor stood up and defended himself, "I

told you that my father and your mother asked me to find some work for April to do in my office when she was suspended from school. That's when I bought her lunches. My father and I visited her at home after she tried to commit suicide. As far as me touching her, I've never touched her inappropriately. And if you are so concerned about your daughter, then why are you trying to get money from me to keep quiet?" He plopped back down and said, "Sounds to me like you are just trying to get some money so that you can keep getting high."

Felicia raised her voice and stated, "For your information, I was going to use the money that I asked you for to get back on my feet. To get my own place again and get my kids away from my mother so she won't be dragging them back to this so-called house of the Lord."

Zachariah hollered, "Okay that's enough." He looked at his new lady friend's daughter and drastically lowered his voice. "Felicia, I know that you have been having a hard time lately. And things are not turning out the way that you think that they should, but if you turn your life over to God, He will give you the answers to all of your problems."

His father went on preaching to her for a few more minutes while Joshua shook his head in disbelief. He couldn't believe that his father was trying to save her right there in his office. It was obvious to Joshua that she was just trying to scare them into giving her money by threatening him with the police.

If only his father could have seen the contempt in her eyes and heard the viciousness in her voice when she first came into his office spouting her demands. Felicia was clearly manipulating the situation between his dad and her mother and was only looking out for herself. He knew that what she was only interested in was getting money to go buy crack. Maybe his dad couldn't see it. But Joshua could see the hunger in her eyes.

He cleared his thoughts and began to pay attention to his father's words again. Joshua was shocked to hear that his father was actually agreeing to give her some money. "I really think that you should wait and see what is going to happen with your criminal case before you uproot the children again. But you are their mother and I want to help you. So find a job and then I will gladly pay the first few months of rent and security deposit for you and the kids."

Felicia shook her head. Looking back and forth between Zachariah and Joshua, she let out a chuckle. Turning very seriously she huffed, "I will go to the police, you know." Her eyes moved between father and son. "I figured the man who was messing around with my underage child wouldn't mind helping us out financially," she paused for clarity, "right now."

The three of them sat in silence for a minute. Joshua noticed his father wringing his hands together like he usually did when he worried. So he interrupted the silence by coolly saying, "I say we don't give her anything. If she goes to the police, fine. If they come and question me, I will just tell them the truth. That this woman just got out of jail because you," he looked at his father, "were nice enough to bail her out. Figuring that we had more money that she could benefit from, she tries to blackmail us to continue her life as a crackhead who neglects her kids."

Felicia raised her eyebrow at Joshua. Then she turned her attention to her elder and asked, "Do you realize what would happen to your church if it got out that the assistant pastor was accused of being a child molester?"

Zachariah leaned in close to her face and said, "We haven't done anything except be kind to you and everyone in your family. But if you want money to keep from going to the police with this crazy lie, then I'll give it to you right out of my own pocket."

Joshua watched in amazement as his father pulled his checkbook out his back pocket and started writing her a check. Felicia turned and stared at him with a smug look on her face. She poured salt in his wound by winking her right eye at him.

When she reached for the check his father held on the other end of it firmly. "Know this, I will never give you any more money after today." Felicia shook her head that she understood. So his father relinquished the check, got up, and exited the room.

Joshua watched his father walk away leaving them alone again. He studied her examining the writing on the check. Satisfied with what she saw, Felicia hopped up out of her chair and left without uttering another word. Once she left with the check, Joshua sat quietly. He was still numb from what just happened. When his office phone rang it made him almost jump out of his skin. Knowing that he was too distracted to handle any church business at that moment, he let the phone go unanswered.

When he called his father into his office for back up, he had expected him to jump to his defense. He figured the two of them could send Felicia slithering away like the snake she was. But his father never had his back on anything that he wanted to do. So Joshua wondered why he thought today would be any different.

He was still in his own world seething when his cell phone rang. He quickly looked to see who it was bothering him now. When he recognized the office number of his real estate agent, he rose from his desk and put on his gray Armani jacket. Joshua wasn't going to waste time calling back. He had instructed his agent to call as soon as he got all of the papers he needed to sign.

Not wanting to have a discussion with his father right then, he left out of the church's side door. What had just happened with Felicia and his father was the final straw for him. Today was the day that he was going to tell his father his plan. Initially, he was going to wait until after the holidays were over to break the news to everyone. But he was too fed up living this lie for even one more day.

Part Three

Whatever Doesn't Kill You Makes You Stronger

30

Felicia couldn't believe that getting the money she asked for had been so easy. She kicked herself for not demanding more than five thousand dollars. Joshua was even bold enough to laugh in her face when she originally asked for the cash. The look on his face when his dad wrote her a check was priceless. At that moment, he wasn't sitting on his high horse looking down his nose at her.

As soon as she walked down the church step she pulled the check out to see what bank Zachariah had an account at. The closest branch was within walking distance so she quickly made her way there before he called her bluff and put a stop payment on the check.

After standing in line for ten minutes she was finally at the front of the line. "Next in line please."

"Hi. I need to cash this check. And can I have two

envelopes please?"

"Sure. Do you have an account with us?" the teller inquired.

"No. I just need the check cashed."

"We could open up an account for you today if you'd like. It only takes a few minutes," the bank employee persisted.

"Not right now. Maybe some other time."

After signing the back of the check and putting a thumbprint on it, Felicia walked away with an envelope full of hundred-dollar bills. Before she left the bank, she moved two of the hundred-dollar bills to the empty envelope. Then she tucked the larger envelope in the small zipper compartment of her purse. The small envelope was to celebrate with Anita and get this monkey off her back. Going cold turkey in jail had her going out of her mind. She thought about getting high twenty-four seven.

Felicia promised herself that she wasn't going to touch the other envelope. That was going to be money to get her life back on track just like she tried to tell them at the church. She would use it to get a lawyer to beat her case and get a new apartment for her and the kids. Felicia was going to show everyone, especially her mother, that despite how her future looked right now, she was going to make something out of herself so her kids could be proud of her.

She didn't know how her life had ended up like this. One day her little family was living a good life and the next everything was spiraling out of control. Her boyfriend Tony had always been very cautious, maybe even paranoid. That's how he was able to keep hustling for as long as he had without ever getting busted by the police. He came home telling her that things were getting bad in the neighborhood because the police were cracking down. Felicia wasn't scared though. Tony always handled the problems that he had with business before. She knew that he would know what to do. He always did.

A few days later, Felicia was jolted awake when she heard a loud thud in the other room. Her eyes got big trying to focus in the dark. The first thing she thought about was being robbed while Tony wasn't home to protect them. She immediately got scared thinking about the safety of her babies. Jumping out of her bed, she hit her funny bone on the corner of the dresser. Felicia covered her mouth and hopped around on one foot in excruciating pain in her attempt not to curse and alert whoever was in their apartment.

The next thing she knew, flashlights were shining in her face and men were screaming at her. She was finally able to figure out that the intruders were the police yelling at her to get down on the ground. Felicia could hear her babies crying and screaming from the other bedrooms.

The police kicked in their apartment door at five o'clock in the morning with a warrant for Tony's arrest. But he was the only one not home. The armed men spent the next hour ransacking the apartment looking for drugs or money while Felicia and her three kids were forced to sit helplessly at the dining room table. One cop stood over her threatening to take the kids to DFAC and lock her in jail if she didn't tell them Tony's whereabouts. When her kids started crying again, she gave in to their demands and called him on his cell phone to ask him to come home. For the first time ever, she hoped that he wouldn't answer her call. And she got her wish.

Felicia and the kids slowly got up when the police finally left. Her whole body began to shake and her eyes filled up with so many tears that she couldn't see in front of her anymore. She cried out, "This isn't right. They can't get away with this. Look what they did to our home."

Brooklyn handed her mom a Kleenex. Felicia wiped her face and walked around surveying their apartment. All of the couch cushions were strewn around the living room and cut open. The kitchen cabinets were all open and the Tupperware bowls were thrown about. The silverware drawer was hanging on for dear life. Before Felicia could push it closed, it slid all the way out making a loud crash as all of the knives, forks, and spoons scattered across the kitchen floor. She cursed and the kids ran in the kitchen to see what was wrong. Felicia remembered Brooklyn stooping down to pick up the silverware, but she told her not to bother.

The four of them stayed together holding hands as they surveyed the rest of the rooms. The men had lifted up all of their mattresses and box springs and moved them off the bed frames. All of the dresser drawers were open and the content was thrown around the rooms. Then Felicia noticed that her purse was upside down in a chair. Everything in it was rummaged through and her wallet was empty. "I don't believe this. They stole my money."

She was in a daze, but heard one of the kids ask, "Mommy, where is daddy?"

Felicia snapped out of her state of shock and called Tony again. His cell phone went directly to voicemail for a second time. She walked out of the room to have some privacy. Then she left him the first of many frantic messages. "Baby where are you? The police were here looking for you.

They have a warrant for your arrest. Please call me back as soon as you hear this so I know that you are okay."

But he didn't call her back. Felicia could understand him not coming home since the police were looking for him. She didn't understand him not letting her know that he was okay though. Figuring that he had gotten arrested after the police left, she called the precinct every day for a week to see if he was in the system. She even called all of the local hospitals in case he was hurt and couldn't call. The day she called his cell phone for what had to be the hundredth time and the number was changed to an unlisted number, she knew that he was gone for good.

Felicia was stuck with three kids and no money coming in. Her emotions were all over the place. One minute she was worried about him and the next she was angry with him for running away without them. Most days, she just wanted to curl up in a ball and die so she could get off the emotional roller coaster she was riding.

She kept hearing her mother's voice haunting her, "I told you so. I told you not to get involved with that boy." Maybe she should have listened to her mother. The two of them didn't have much in common, but maybe her mother was actually trying to save her from following in her footsteps. Felicia remembered her daddy being gone a lot at night when she was little. She felt sorry for her mother sitting up worrying about if or when he would make it home safely. And then she ended up doing the exact same thing with Anthony.

During her sleepless nights, every noise she heard, from the faucet dripping in the bathroom to the refrigerator humming in the kitchen kept her awake thinking. She had always been curious about the crack that Tony sold. It had to be the best feeling in the world because customers were falling all over themselves to get it. Not only did Tony come home with a lot of money, but he also came home with some great stuff from time to time. She was wearing a beautiful one karat diamond ring that one of his customers traded right off his wife's finger so that he could keep getting high when his money ran out. Then there was the time Tony came home one night with a brand-new DVD player that was still in the box. A DVD player for a twenty-dollar rock was a good deal every once in a while to keep his customers coming back. At the time, she thought that it was their loss and her family's gain.

One night, when the loud silence and missing her man got the best of Felicia, she left the kids at home asleep to pay Anita a visit. She was one of Tony's regular customers. So Felicia headed to her apartment hoping that she had heard from him. He still hadn't come home and never returned her calls. But maybe he was still selling to his long-term customers. Felicia was desperate and felt like she didn't have anything to lose by going there.

"Hey. What's up?" Anita looked around then stared her visitor directly in the face from her doorway.

"I'm looking for Tony. You heard from him lately?"

Anita squinted and looked Felicia up and down. "Come inside." She moved out of the way so Felicia could enter and quickly locked the door behind her. "I ain't seen him. I've been calling, but he hasn't picked up."

Felicia looked around at the apartment. Anita didn't have anything worth writing home about. She didn't have a stereo or DVD player, just a small TV with a thick layer of dust across the screen. The door to the next room was closed so Felicia couldn't see beyond that. There was only one glass on the coffee table so Felicia assumed that she was alone. She did smell a weird smell in the air that she hadn't smelled before. Felicia wondered if she had interrupted Anita doing something.

"You don't know where he is?" Anita curiously asked.

"No. I think he is laying low because the police are looking for him." Felicia threw her hand up in the air and frowned. "I don't know. I thought maybe you'd heard from him since you buy from him all the time."

"You sound like you're wearing a wire or something."

Felicia looked at Anita like she had three heads. "What?"

"You see me in the street and barely speak. Now you show up at my door looking for Tony. What you expect me to think?"

Felicia was insulted but thought about it for a second. Then she slowly lifted up her shirt and turned around in a circle to ease Anita's fears.

Anita continued to stare at her suspiciously.

"Look, I am looking for Tony." She paused and lowered her voice a little. "But that's not the only reason why I'm here."

"Okay. Well spit it out. Why else are you here?"

"Um, I um," Felicia hesitated. She rocked back and forth where she stood noticing that Anita crossed her arms. "I've got a lot on my mind. I had a couple drinks, but I think I need something stronger. I was hoping that maybe you could help me out."

She threw her head back and smiled. "You got any money?"

"A little."

Anita walked away from Felicia toward her bedroom shaking her head and laughing. Felicia was getting angry. She wanted to know what was so funny but decided to keep her mouth shut for now. Anita returned a few seconds later with a towel. "Lucky for you, I had some already. But you've got the next round."

Both ladies sat down on the couch. The cushion was a lot flatter than it looked. Felicia felt like she was sitting on the ground. But once again she chose to keep her mouth shut not to offend Anita. She watched Anita carefully unroll the dirty towel revealing a saucer with a razor blade, a foggy glass pipe with a piece of steel wool at one end of it, a cheap lighter, and a small piece of crack on it. "Is this what you want?"

Felicia didn't take her eyes off the saucer when she replied, "Yes. But I need you to show me what to do."

Anita shook her head as a smirk appeared on her face. That was the night Felicia and Anita became friends. After that, Felicia spent more time hanging out at Anita's than she did at her own apartment. When Felicia and Anita weren't getting high, they were coming up with schemes to get money so they could get high again.

Eventually, Felicia became ashamed of what she was doing and didn't want her kids to see her. So she stayed away more nights than she was home, leaving them to fend for themselves. What started out as drinking and smoking to get her mind off Tony and all of her problems, had turned into something that she had to do daily to survive. She couldn't control her craving. Felicia was always trying to get the same rush that she got from her very first hit that night. But she never did. When she ate and then got high later, she threw up. So she stopped eating. It wasn't long before her pants got so loose that she had to fold the waistband down twice or wear a big belt so they didn't fall right off of her. After a while she didn't care how her hair or nails looked or what people thought about her like she used to. All she cared about was getting high. When her brain was tingling and she was soaring above it all, she didn't have a care in the world.

Now that she had some money courtesy of Pastor, she headed to Anita's. After the horrible experience she'd had the last few months, Felicia just wanted to feel good again. At least for a little while.

31

Mary wasn't sure why Zachariah had asked her to come up to the church and talk to him on a day that she wasn't scheduled to work. She was at home bringing down boxes of Christmas decorations from the attic when he called. Since she had her hands full, she was tempted to just let the phone ring. But she decided against it in case it was one of the kid's schools calling about an emergency.

She didn't understand what was so urgent. But since he sounded so upset, she jumped in her car and rushed to Mt. Zion. When she arrived, she knocked on his office door, but he didn't answer. Mary slowly opened the door anyway to wait on him. To her surprise, he was in his office after all. Not only did he look upset, he looked ill. His eyes and nose looked red and his forehead was shiny from sweating. He was just staring at pictures on his bookcase deep in thought.

Obviously, he had not heard her knock on the door. Mary didn't want to startle him by speaking, so she quietly walked over to an empty chair, sat down, and waited. It took him a full minute to even notice that there was someone in the room with him. A slight smile crossed his face. But even from where Mary was sitting, she could see that he had been crying. Zachariah was a manly man. She couldn't imagine him crying unless something horrible had happened.

Mary quickly asked, "What's wrong, honey? Did somebody die?" She regretted blurting out the question as soon as she thought about how impersonal that must have sounded.

Zachariah tried to smile again and answered, "No, baby. Nobody passed away today."

She apologized, "I'm sorry. I didn't mean for it to come out that way." Mary paused for a second to give him a chance to explain to her what was going on. When he didn't offer any information she asked, "Are you going to tell me why you had me drop everything and hurry over here?"

Zachariah took a deep breath, grinned, and said, "Sorry. It's been a rough day so far. Joshua and I had an unexpected visitor here this morning."

Mary interrupted, "Who?"

He held up his hand and almost whispered, "Mary, all of this is hard enough for me to tell you without you interrupting me." She stared at him with a puzzled look on her face. Then she sat all the way back in her seat determined to be attentive and not interrupt him again.

Zachariah started his story of the day's events again. "Felicia was our visitor. It seems that she believes that Joshua has acted inappropriately towards April." Mary's head jerked back and her eyebrows came together. But she didn't say anything so he continued. He firmly stated, "She claimed that April confided in her that Joshua touches her."

Mary covered her mouth and mumbled, "Oh my God."

"Of course Joshua insisted that this is all a big lie. Then Felicia threatened to go to the police unless we gave her some money. She said the money would be so she could move her kids out of your house so you couldn't bring April back to Mt. Zion anymore."

Mary's eyes filled up with tears and she couldn't keep quiet anymore. Her voice was shaky when she asked, "So are you telling me that Felicia says that Joshua is touching April?" She had to pause to clear her throat. "And she came in here blackmailing him?" Mary just looked at Zachariah nodding his head. She couldn't believe any of this. But it must be true. Why would he lie on Felicia after he spent all that money bailing her out of jail?

When Mary woke up this morning, Felicia was already gone. She wasn't sure if she had even slept in the house at all. So she asked Anthony, "Did your mother sleep with you?" But he said that she hadn't. She checked the living room for any sign that her daughter had slept on the couch, but there wasn't any. The thought of her child running the streets getting high crossed her mind, but she quickly dismissed it. *Felicia was in jail long enough for the drugs to get out of her system. She wouldn't be stupid enough to start again, or would she?*

Mary was so tired from her normal routine with the kids, plus taking care of paying the bail, running back and forth to the jail waiting for Felicia to be released that she went to bed once her daughter was safely at home with her kids. She now regretted the fact that she hadn't paid closer attention to her daughter's first night out or offered the other half of her bed to her. Some would say that you're never too old to sleep with your mama.

Sitting in Zachariah's office, Mary thought back to Joshua's birthday party. April had been so anxious to go with her. Mary's hand started shaking and she hollered, "What the hell is going on?" Then she immediately covered her mouth when she realized that she was cursing in the Lord's house. "Lord, please forgive me."

Even though Zachariah was physically in bad shape himself, he got up to comfort her. Mary held on to him for a few seconds of comfort, but then pushed him away. She wiped her face and demanded, "Finish the story, please."

He sat down on the edge of his desk, still facing her, and held her hand. "Joshua was convinced that she would just use the money to get high. I only gave in to her because I didn't want her going to the police with a lie like that. So I wrote her a check."

Mary was scared to ask but did it anyway. "For how much?"

Zachariah took a deep breath, "For what she asked for; five thousand dollars."

Mary reached for the small gold cross that rested on her neck.

The two of them heard the office door creak behind them. They turned around at the same time to find Joshua standing there. "Hey. I needed to talk to you Dad." His eyes traveled to Mary. "But I guess we can talk later."

Zachariah let go of Mary's hand, rose from the desk, and stopped him as he turned to go. "No. It's okay, son. I was just telling Mary what happened." Joshua slowly turned back around. "Look I realize that what I did this morning, may have given you the impression that I doubted you," Zachariah paused to make sure that his son was really paying him attention. "I hope that you know that I don't think that you are capable of doing anything like that. But I also think that Felicia might be able to get some fool in the media, trying to make a name for themself, to take her seriously. You know how hard we worked to build this church." He outstretched his arms and continued, "And I can't have some liar taking it all away from us."

Mary fidgeted in her chair. She wondered if Zachariah forgot that she was sitting right there while he talked badly about her family? Feeling very uncomfortable sitting in the midst of their conversation, she attempted to get up and leave the office.

Joshua put up his hand, "You may as well stay, Mary. What I have to say won't take long." She looked up at Joshua curiously and slid back down in her seat. He took a deep breath and announced, "I hope you were finished, Dad. I feel another one of your "this-is-going-to-be-all-yours" speeches coming and I can't take another one of those."

Mary's eyes darted from Zachariah standing with his arms outstretched like Fred Sanford from the hit seventies sitcom Sanford & Son to Joshua. She could see Joshua's shoulders slightly moving up and down because he was breathing so hard. And Zachariah was staring so intensely at his son because of his harsh tone that she wanted to run for cover.

Joshua was gifted with a deep manly voice in his early teenage years. But Mary had never heard him speak harsh to his father like this before. "Yes, you have worked hard to build this church. So hard that you left your own wife in the hands of nurses while she was dying so that you wouldn't miss out on anything going on here. You spend more time with your sick and shut-in members than you did with Mom when she was sick and shut in."

Zachariah pointed one of his fingers toward Joshua and demanded, "Son, I think you need to stop before you say something that you are going to regret."

"You wanna know what I regret? I regret not making you listen to me. This church makes you happy, Dad. You chose this life. Mom even chose this life when she married you. I didn't choose this life. It was forced on me. I've been trying to tell you that for years, but you don't listen to me." He let out a nervous laugh. "Do you know how many times I've heard that I couldn't do something that I wanted to do because I was a preacher's kid? I just can't keep living like this, Dad."

"Most people would love to live like you son. You live in a three hundred-thousand-dollar house. Drive a Porsche. Dress nice. You always have money in your pocket and have a beautiful fiancée." Zachariah raised his voice to match his son's. "Living like what son?"

"Unhappy," Joshua shouted and pounded his fist against the wall. Mary and Zachariah both jumped. "You are going to have to get someone else to be your assistant pastor, because I am resigning. I can stay until the end of the year if you want. But I'm sure that you won't have any problem finding a suitable replacement for me."

Zachariah held up his hand again for Joshua to stop talking. "Did you just say a suitable replacement for you? How can I find a substitute for my son?" Mary could hear the desperation in his voice. "Joshua, don't let what happened earlier today make you do something rash."

Joshua threw up his hands up in frustration. "You're still not listening to me Dad. This is bigger than what happened today. It's what has been happening all my life every time I try and tell you what I want. And it's about time for me to put a stop to it. I have a right to be happy too."

He moved towards his father's office door to leave. As if it was an afterthought, he announced, "I know that you won't approve, but I just bought a place in Stone Mountain. When I'm finished remodeling, it will be a nice jazz supper club. I would love for you to come by and see it. But if you don't want to, I understand." Joshua walked out and slammed the door behind him leaving his father dazed.

Mary was truly blown away with all of this disturbing news. She didn't want to abandon Zachariah, but she really wanted to leave and go check on her own family. Mary absentmindedly uttered, "Don't worry. I'm sure that he was just upset. When he calms down, he'll be back." She grabbed his hand and squeezed it. But her body betrayed her and she looked away when their eyes met.

He squeezed back and honestly admitted, "No, I don't think he'll be back."

Zachariah let go of her hand. Mary could hear his breathing getting louder. "Baby, you don't look so good," she reluctantly admitted.

"I've been hurting since Felicia left earlier." He grabbed his chest and tried to go back to his chair on the other side of his oversized desk.

His mouth was moving, but Mary couldn't understand him. The next thing she knew, he had dropped down to his knees. Mary tried to grab him and keep him from falling to the floor, but he was too heavy so they both toppled over. She looked up and pleaded, “Sweet Jesus, no don’t do this to me again Lord.” Mary pulled herself together and snatched the phone off the hook to call 911. When the emergency operator came on the line Mary yelled, “Please send an ambulance to Mt. Zion Baptist Church. I think the pastor is having a heart attack!”

32

"Mr. Williams suffered a mild heart attack. So we're going to keep him here for observation. He should be well enough to go home in a couple days, but he will need your support to stay well. He needs to keep away from stressful situations, exercise more, and change his diet. I will have a nutritionist speak to him about what specific foods to refrain from eating." The doctor glanced at his Rolex and announced, "I will be back to check on him later on." Then he abruptly walked away without asking Mary or David if they had any questions for him.

It wasn't long before the hospital room filled up with visitors. When two of the church deacons showed up to visit Zachariah, David stayed in the room with them to answer their questions and make sure his father didn't get worked up. Mary excused herself and used this as an opportunity to try and reach Joshua again.

She went back to the closest payphone. Her call went straight to voicemail for the forth times. After that, she made a few calls and was finally able to track down Tracy's cell phone number. Each call took longer than she anticipated because word had already gotten out that an ambulance had driven away from Mt. Zion Baptist Church with their beloved pastor in the back. Mary had to assure each person that Zachariah was going to be okay and that she wasn't calling with bad news.

Finally, Mary dialed Tracy's number and anxiously waited for her to answer. "Hello."

"Hi Tracy, this is Mary Lewis from the church."

"Oh, hi Sister Lewis." Mary could hear the uncertainty in the woman's voice. So she got right to the reason for her call.

"Tracy, I'm sorry to bother you, but I'm looking for Joshua."

"You're looking for Josh?"

"Yes. Pastor had a heart attack. David and I have been trying to reach your fiancé ever since."

"Oh my God. Is he gonna be okay?"

"Yes. David, the deacons, and I are all at the hospital with him. The doctor says that he needs to change some things in his life, but he will be fine if he does what he is supposed to do."

"Do you know what happened to make Pastor have a heart attack?"

Mary couldn't hold the tears back any longer. Both of the ladies were quiet for a moment. Tracy waited while Mary got herself together.

Once she dried her eyes and loudly blew her nose,

she sighed. Mary whispered, "Like Pastor told me, it's been a rough day." Mary grinned to relieve some of her discomfort. "It's a close race between my child and his child as to which one of them put him in that hospital bed," she confessed.

"You mean Josh?" Tracy interrupted.

"Yes. You know, Zachariah gave me the money to bail my foolish child out of jail and apparently she repaid him by accusing Joshua of touching my granddaughter, April, in all the wrong places." Mary let out a nervous laugh. "Joshua was very upset that his dad gave Felicia money to shut her up. And then he announced that he was quitting his job as assistant pastor."

"What?" Tracy exclaimed. "All this happened today?"

"Yes. David started calling Joshua on his cell phone right after this happened, but he hasn't called back. So have you talked to him?"

"No, I haven't seen him or talked to him. He isn't taking my calls either."

Mary let out a deep breath in frustration. "Well, when you talk to him, please tell him that his dad is sick and he needs to call me or his brother."

"I will. I'm sorry all of this is happening Sister Lewis. I'll talk to you later."

David spent the rest of the day at the hospital with Mary and Zachariah. Mary could tell that this situation had him stressed out. Not only was his dad in the hospital, but he was also worried about his brother. He finally announced, "When I leave here, I'm gonna go find Joshua. I don't know what his problem is. Throwing a temper tantrum like a little girl and then disappearing."

Mary couldn't even find the words to respond. The only other thing she had on her mind besides the health of her man, was dealing with her daughter and granddaughter. When visiting hours were over, they both reluctantly left Zachariah's side to set out on their separate missions.

She was grateful that David was quiet in the car maneuvering his way through traffic as he gave her a ride home. She needed a few minutes to think. *Had Joshua really done anything to April? Why would she say that he did if he really didn't? Felicia had to be behind all this. Had she been so desperate to get high that she made all this up? We've all been through so much lately. When is all this craziness going to end?*

33

Mary walked in the door to her house that evening ordering her youngest grandkids to bed. They whined in unison, “But it’s not even our bedtime yet.” The way she stopped taking her jacket off and whipped around to face them after their disrespectful response to her command, caused them to change their tune. They both quickly shuffled off to bed with their heads held down mumbling under their breath.

April turned the TV off and tried to make a run for cover. “Not so fast young lady.” She slowly turned to face her grandmother who asked, “Is your mother here?”

“No ma’am.”

Mary couldn’t remember the last time April used ma’am without being instructed to do so first.

She continued to pull off her jacket. Then she sat

down on the loveseat and patted the cushion right next to her. "Come sit down next to me. We need to talk," she insisted in a nicer voice.

April sat down and sighed. Before Mary could figure out how to start the conversation April said, "Grandma, I really need to go and do my homework. I started making dinner like you asked me to and I was so busy watching the kids, I forgot to do it." Mary wasn't fooled by her granddaughter's attempt to win brownie points for cooking dinner alone and trying to get out of talking to her.

"Why are you so anxious to do your homework? Any other time, you swear that your teachers didn't give you any."

April didn't even bother responding.

Her grandmother firmly tried to pull her back down by the arm when she tried to ease up off the love seat. "I'll write a note to your teacher explaining why you couldn't do your homework. We need to have a conversation about something very important."

April yanked her arm away from her and pulled up her sleeve to examine four deep nail impressions. Her grandmother closed her eyes for a second. Then she said, "I'm so sorry. I didn't know that I grabbed you that hard."

Mary watched as she rubbed her arm to give it some relief.

"Tell me what's going on, April."

"I dunno whatcha talking about," April said with an attitude.

"Tell me what you and your mother talked about when she came home the other night."

April shrugged. "Nothing," she quickly answered.

"Nothing? You hadn't seen your mother in a few months and you didn't talk about anything?"

April looked up at the ceiling. "Um. She asked me about school."

Mary exhaled out of frustration. "Baby, what did you say to your mother to make her accuse Joshua Williams of molesting you?"

Someone sucked all of the air out of the room. "Huh?" escaped from April's mouth. Mary could see her body start to shake. Then she blurted out, "I told her the truth."

Mary refused to believe that. Her nose began to flare. "Did your mother put you up to this?"

April jumped to her feet and yelled, "No, my mother didn't put me up to this. He did it."

"Did what, April? What exactly did he do?"

April turned away and started pacing the floor. "I already went through all of this with Mama. She said she would take care of it."

"Really? Well did she say she was going to call and make you a doctor's appointment?"

April stopped moving. "Make me an appointment for what?"

"To make sure that you are okay."

April shook her head.

"Well, when is she taking you to the police station?"

"For what? Why do we need to go there?"

Mary patted the cushion next to her again. Slowly, she walked back and returned to her seat. "You need to go see a doctor and get examined. And then you need to go report him to the police."

April's mumbled, "I'm fine. I don't need to go to the doctor." Mary watched her holding on to her arm looking down at the floor.

Mary exhaled. "If your mother isn't back in the morning, then I'll take you to the police precinct myself." she announced as she struggled to get up off the couch.

April stood up too and managed to say, "I don't want to cause any problems, Grandma."

She turned around to face her granddaughter and rested her hand on her full hips. "It's much too late for that young lady."

April's eyebrow went up.

"Do you know where I've been all day?"

April shook her head but avoided eye contact.

"I was with Pastor Williams. He had a heart attack because of all of this." Mary emphasized each word as she stated, "Do you realize that he could have died?" Her words made April sit back down on the love seat. She kept pushing. "Has your mother been back here?"

"No. I haven't seen her."

"Humph. Well she made a beeline to the church to ask Joshua for money. She told him if he didn't give her money, then she was going to tell everyone that he molested you. Does that sound like a concerned mother to you?"

April rolled her eyes. "How much did he give her?"

"Joshua didn't give her anything."

Mary could see April's wheels spinning. "Well if he didn't give her any money then where is she?"

"Joshua didn't give her any money. But Pastor did. He paid her to keep the reputation of his church safe." Mary let out a big breath, shut her eyes, and shook her head. Then she blurted out, "Your mother went to the church to help herself not you. She left the church with five thousand dollars. I hate to say it, but you and I both know what she is doing with that money right now."

The two of them were quiet mulling over what was just said.

"Baby, tell me exactly what Joshua did to you," Mary gently requested.

April remained quiet. The only noise she made was the faint sound of her chewing on the inside of her bottom lip. "He -- Grandma, I'm not comfortable talking to you about this."

"Well, no one else is here trying to help you but me, April."

"Mama usually doesn't stay away for more than a few days. She'll be back soon."

They sat listening to the wind rattle the windows of the house. April looked toward the front door when she thought she heard the screen door open. Mary looked back at the door for a second too before she whispered, "She's not coming."

"Huh?"

"If you are looking for your mother, I don't think she is coming. But I'm here. And no matter what, I'm not going anywhere. But I need you to talk to me so I can help you." Mary sat back down and rubbed April's hand. "Are you sure your mother didn't put you up to this?"

April shook her head and wiped the tear that had finally escaped that was running down her face with her free hand. "Is Pastor going to be okay? I never meant to hurt him."

Mary tilted her head and her eyes squinted. "Who did

you mean to hurt?"

April snatched her hand away and stood up. "I'm sleepy. I'm 'bout to go to bed."

Mary patted her hands on her lap and stood to her feet too. "Well first thing in the morning, we are going to the police station to file a complaint against Joshua."

"What's gonna happen after that?"

"They will ask you a bunch of questions. Then probably ask him a bunch of questions. Maybe he will get arrested. I'm sure we'll have to go to court at some point." She exhaled. "I don't know baby."

April walked away without replying with her head hung low.

34

Mary hardly got any sleep last night. She tossed and turned, worrying about whether April had really been molested in some way by Joshua. All this time she believed that he had a positive effect on her grandchild. During the two weeks that she was suspended from school, April seemed to look forward to working at the church. Mary thought having her at Mt. Zion everyday instead of giving her a mountain of chores at home was a good move. Now, she questioned that decision. Joshua had blindsided everyone with his sudden decision to quit, but she never pegged him as a predator.

Why didn't April tell me? She had plenty of opportunities to confide in me. I know she gets mad at me when I punish her for doing stupid stuff. But I thought we were getting along better, especially when we spend time cooking together. Why would she wait until her mother came home to tell her? And where did I go wrong with Felicia to make her act the way she does? Who neglects her kids and cuts off ties with her parents? Then blackmails the man who hasn't seen her in years but still bailed her out of jail as a favor to her mother who is taking care of her kids?

Mary was also very concerned about Zachariah's health. He was stubborn and set in his ways. Getting him to eliminate stress, start exercising, and eating right wasn't going to be an easy task. But that might not even be her problem anymore. If his son actually did hurt her granddaughter, what did that mean for their relationship? She hated to be selfish at a time like this, but she had fallen in love with him. He was a good man and she would be devastated if she had to stop seeing him. This was one big nightmare.

Her alarm clock told her that it was almost time to get out of bed and wake the kids up for school. That also meant that she would have to follow through with her threat and drive April to the police station. This was one of those rare days where she didn't look forward to getting up and facing the world. So she stayed there a little longer and prayed for guidance.

"Why does April always get to miss school?" Anthony asked in an irritated tone.

"April and I have to go somewhere to go first," Mary explained as she dropped him off at school. "I'll be back up here to drop her off in a little while. Now hurry up and get in there so you won't be late."

She watched her grandkids sneer at each other before April finally rolled her eyes and looked away. Anthony finally stomped up the school stairs as she slowly pulled away from the curb. Mary could see April look longingly at the side mirror watching her school get smaller in the distance.

They drove all the way to the police station in complete silence. Mary found a spot and parked. Neither one of them reached for their door handle though. Mary finally said, "Come on. Let's get out."

"Wait."

"What did you say?" Mary quickly asked.

April hesitated, but confessed, "He never touched me."

Mary shut her eyes, threw her right hand up in the air, and whispered, "Thank you Jesus." She let out a deep sigh of relief and stared at April. She had her head hung low and her eyes shut tight. "Well, why did you tell us that he did, April?"

April shrugged her shoulder and bit her bottom lip.

Mary quickly lost her patience and repeated her question much louder this time.

April got loud too. "Because I liked him. I thought he was cool, but I overheard him talking about my family. He was talking about Daddy being a drug dealer who left us and Mama being a crackhead. I'm tired of people talking bad about my parents all the time." Her eyes met her grandmother's. "Then he said that I have some serious issues and that he was stuck babysitting me because his dad was trying to impress you."

"That's no reason to lie and try to ruin the man's life, April," Mary hollered.

April blurted out, "I knew you were gonna take his side. Mama always said Mt. Zion had you brainwashed."

Mary leaned in closer. “What did you say?”

“Mama said that when my granddaddy died, she came and asked you for money. Daddy was gone and we needed help. But you wouldn’t give it to her. She said that you made us go without so that you could give all your money to the church.”

The word brainwashed made Mary indignant. It offended her that she tried to bring up her family right in the church and Felicia thought that she was brainwashed. Mary couldn’t hold back her retort. “I’d rather be brainwashed for the Lord than be a crackhead that can’t take care of her kids like your mother.” She regretted the words as soon as they passed her lips.

Mary put her head in her hands and tried to regain control of her emotions. When she turned back to April, she was rocking back and forth like she was about to explode. “Listen baby. I shouldn’t have said that. But I am not brainwashed.” Mary paused trying to decide if she should explain what happened. She quickly decided that April heard her mom’s version of what happened. Now it was time for the truth. “Your mother came to me when I was grieving about losing my husband. I hadn’t seen her in months. She didn’t come to her own father’s funeral to say goodbye to him or come check on the woman that gave birth to her. But she showed up two weeks later talking about how she knew the insurance company gave me some money and she wanted her part of it. Staring at her with her messed up hair, disheveled clothes, and a strange look in her eyes, I knew that something was wrong. I just didn’t know what at the time. So I said no. And she told me that I would never see my grandkids again and stormed out the house.”

April tilted her head and her eyebrows scrunched up. Mary continued, "Just so you know, I used the small insurance check I got to fix my house. The house is old and it was falling apart. Several of the kitchen cabinets were broken so I treated myself to a nice kitchen remodel and got my leaky roof fixed. I did not give away my money to the church." Mary shook her head and exhaled. She was still trying to calm down from the insult. "And I'm not taking his side. Do you really think I would ever choose anyone or anything over you? You are my family. I love you and your brother and sister. But right is right and wrong is wrong. Joshua should have never said those mean things about you, but you shouldn't have started this horrible lie."

She watched April squirm for a few moments. Then she finally confessed, "I know what I said was wrong. I'm just tired of the way everyone treats me like crap. But I didn't mean for things to get so out of control." This was the first time April showed any signs of remorse. Mary was ready for this nightmare to be over so she reached across the armrest and grabbed April's hand.

"Baby, you are a smart young lady. But as you can see, you can't control how people act. You can only control how you act. That being said, there is no excuse for the way either of your parents have abandoned and neglected you. They will surely have to answer to God for that. But you cannot let that ruin your life by continuing to act out. If you do, the next time we are at the police station it could be because someone is pressing charges against you. You can't keep fighting everyone that hurts your feelings April."

April exhaled and looked up. "I know Grandma. I'm really gonna to try and control my temper. I don't want to end up in jail."

"Can I tell you something else?"

April smiled and shook her head.

"You are also a beautiful young lady and because of that boys are going to show you a lot of attention. But boys come and go, but your education is something that will stay with you. I know about all those days you missed from school last year. Were you cutting school to be with Brandon?"

April stared straight ahead out the front windshield. When a tear rolled down the side of her cheek Mary had her answer. She wiggled her hand free so she could wipe it away.

Mary continued, "Brandon has moved on to another girl and you are stuck repeating the eight-grade. Please, I'm begging you, stop worrying about boys right now. You have plenty of time for them when you get older. Hit your books, sing your heart out in the church choir, help your grandmother cook up the best food in Atlanta, and just enjoy being a kid while you can."

"Yes ma'am."

"That's good enough for me," Mary said as she let out a huge sigh of relief and reached for her first-born grandchild.

They stayed in the parking lot hugging for a minute. Mary released her and warned, "You aren't exactly off the hook young lady. You have a couple of people that you owe some really big apologies to." That's when the dam broke and the stored-up tears freely flowed down April's face and she sobbed like a baby.

April and Mary spent a little while longer talking in the car. She wanted to make sure that her granddaughter was okay before she dropped her off at school. Now that Mary knew for sure that April hadn't been molested, she could head back to the hospital to check on Zachariah.

Mary didn't know what she would do if she lost another man from her life. She spent the day fussing over Zachariah making sure that he ate all his food, did his breathing treatment, and was comfortable. He kept insisting that he was fine and wanted to rest at home. Of course, she couldn't make that happen. But she suspected that he was trying to get back to work at the church. He was putting on a good act of feeling okay. But he slept a lot. That let her know that he was exhausted. It was painful for Mary to see Zachariah lying in a hospital bed so weak after watching him be strong all these years.

After going home to make sure the kids did their homework and had a home cooked meal for dinner, she arranged for a girl friend to spend the night with the kids. Then Mary gladly returned to the hospital to spend her first night with Zachariah. It wasn't what she had envisioned. Instead of the two of them wrapped up in each other's arms all night on their honeymoon, he was lying in his elevated hospital bed at Emory University Hospital snoring away while she tossed and turned on a tiny pullout bed right next to him. And every couple of hours when a nurse came in to check on him, Mary found herself wide awake again.

35

Ever since Joshua stormed out of his father's church on Friday, he had been avoiding everyone. He'd gotten several calls from the church, his brother, and Tracy. Mary had even been blowing up his phone. Instead of answering his cell, when he recognized their numbers, he just let them go to voicemail. Since he wasn't ready to hear them lecture him about wanting to leave Mt. Zion. He didn't even bother to listen to his messages.

He knew that if he went home, he would have to face Tracy. When his mother died, he was at the lowest point in his life. He didn't want to be alone because if he was, his mind would wander back to missing her. Joshua was so depressed that he didn't want to leave his house much. Tracy was a great girlfriend. So she supported him when he was down by being there for whatever he needed around the clock. For a while, it was nice having someone to cook dinner every night for him. She spent so much time at his place when he was in mourning that it didn't make sense to keep paying rent for a place she never slept at. The next thing he knew Tracy sweet talked him into letting her move in with him after a long session of making love. Right now, he regretted that decision as well as so many others he had made in his life. Since he wasn't ready to deal with her either, he decided that calling the house voice mail and leaving a message directly on the system instead of calling the house was easier. "Hey, I need some time to be alone and clear my head. I'll see you in a few days."

Joshua was hoping that his generic voice mail would be the thing to push Tracy over the edge. He wanted her to be so fed up with him that she would leave on her own. If not, then he would have to make her realize that it was really over and force her to move out of his house.

On his way to check himself into a nice hotel in Buckhead, Joshua realized that he didn't have anything but the clothes on his back. He remembered the pair of running shoes that he kept in his trunk for emergencies and cursed himself for not keeping an outfit in there too. Pulling into Lenox Square Mall's parking lot solved this problem. At the mall, he purchased a few casual outfits, some underwear, and a designer travel case. It contained a toothbrush, toothpaste, and a hairbrush. He even picked up some Godiva Chocolate to snack on and a couple food magazines to read.

An hour later, he had checked himself into the Atlanta Marriott Marquis carrying shopping bags instead of suitcases. Upstairs in his suite, he looked out to a view of the activity of downtown Atlanta. He presumed that no one would find him if they were looking for him.

It was a luxury hotel with all the amenities that he needed to relax. So he stopped looking out the window at all the midday hustle and bustle that he was trying to get away from. Joshua decided to kick back on his king size bed, watch some cable, and order room service. He spent the rest of the day reading the newest issues of Food & Wine and Bon Appétit, eating a gourmet cheeseburger, drinking wine, and watching movies.

It was nice to be away from Tracy, his dad, Mt. Zion, and have a chance to kick his feet up. His only distraction was his cell phone, because it kept ringing. Finally, he cut it off all together so he didn't have to think about it.

He never got to sleep in late on the weekends at home. Tracy always had something for them to do on Saturdays and there was church on Sundays. So Joshua made sure that the expensive drapes were completely closed to block the morning sunlight. When he woke up early anyway out of habit, he remembered why it was dark in his suite. He rolled over and went back to sleep. When he finally got up around noon, Joshua decided to venture out of his room for the first time. After he showered and shaved, he found the hotel's sports bar and ordered lunch and a glass of beer. He walked around the lovely hotel admiring its lobby, atrium, and fitness center. After his food digested, he took advantage of the exercise equipment and the indoor pool.

While enjoying a massage, it occurred to him that he should do the right thing and return his family's calls. He quickly dismissed that idea figuring that he would have to face them soon enough. Joshua had already decided not to attend church the next day. It would be the first time in years that he would miss church service. But he wanted to let his father know that he was serious and wasn't speaking out of anger.

Joshua thought about hitting one of the many popular bars in the neighborhood that night. Inviting one of the many women who flirted with him up to his suite even crossed his mind. But it didn't take long for him to push that thought to the side. He wanted to get away from his old ways and focus on his future. So he decided to take this time to initiate setting up his new website for his supper club.

When he checked in on Friday, he requested a late checkout. Finally leaving his hideaway Sunday afternoon feeling accomplished, he headed home. Tracy hadn't made it in from church yet. Grateful that she must have made a stop before coming home, he relaxed. When he went to the fridge for a glass of water, he found a note from her stuck to it. It read, "Joshua, if you get home before I get back, everyone has been trying to reach you because your father had a heart attack on Friday. He is at Emory University Hospital. But I am picking him up after church and bringing him to our house so we can take care of him since David and his wife have a new baby to take care of. Please don't leave. We need to talk."

He dropped his cell phone as soon as he picked it up. When he picked it up again, his mind drew a blank. He couldn't remember anyone's phone number. After a few jittery seconds Joshua got himself together to get the number to the hospital. By the time he finally got connected to the correct floor, he was told that his father had already been released. He knew better than to be rude, but he hung up in the woman's ear anyway.

Guilt suddenly overwhelmed him. It never occurred to him that his dad would take the news that he was quitting so hard. On top of that, he was in a fancy hotel ignoring his family's numerous calls on purpose while his father could have been dying.

After pacing the floor and looking out the picture window in the front room several times for Tracy's car, Joshua went to the bathroom to wipe his forehead. It was now dripping with sweat like he had run ten miles. He looked at himself in the mirror and was disgusted. "You selfish bastard," he hissed at the face staring back at him.

The sound of car doors slamming in the driveway startled him. He ran back through the kitchen and out the front door. David and Tracy were trying to help his father out of the car. But Zachariah was fighting them all the way. He hollered, "Stop treating me like a baby. I don't need your help." The two of them backed away trying to keep him calm.

All three of them froze when they noticed Joshua rapidly approaching them. Since he parked his car in the garage, he suddenly realized that they weren't expecting him to be home. Joshua gave his dad a big hug and said, "We are going to take good care of you, Dad. The guest room bed is very comfortable. I know because I've had to sleep on it a couple times when Tracy was mad at me." He smiled at his attempt of humor to lighten the mood, but he was the only one.

Sensing the tension between the four of them, Joshua said, "Well, let's get inside because it's cold out here." He stepped back and let his family go ahead of him. None of them said a word to him and that hurt worse than if they had all cursed him out.

Inside he heard Tracy say, "Dad, let me show you to your room. We already brought some of your clothes over from your house." Joshua closed his eyes and shook his head. Tracy seemed more comfortable with his family than he was.

As they slowly walked up the stairs, Joshua could hear his father fussing. "I hope that you didn't bring too much of my stuff over here. To ease everyone's mind, I'll stay here a couple of days. But I'm not a child you know. And I can take care of myself."

Once Tracy and his dad were out of hearing range, David grumbled, "That was pretty lousy the way you broke your news to Dad and then made yourself unavailable for two days. If I thought Dad was able to handle it, I would kick your ass right here in your own house."

Before Joshua could recover from the shock and respond, his brother was already headed upstairs to say goodbye to their father. Thirty minutes later, his brother was gone, his father was upstairs taking a nap, and Tracy was in the kitchen cooking Sunday dinner. Joshua joined her in the kitchen to break the silence. "Who preached today's sermon?"

Tracy dryly answered, "Since we couldn't find you," she turned and gave him a dirty look, "Your brother asked your dad's friend, Pastor Thomas, from Macon to be the guest preacher."

Joshua shook his head up and down in approval. He knew that Minister Thomas was riveting enough to have everyone up on their feet shouting. Sensing the anger that she felt for him, he figured this was as good a time as any to break the news to her.

"I guess you know what happened by now." He hesitated before continuing. "Look, I know that I shouldn't have disappeared, but I really did need to be alone. I can't be who my father wants me to be. I have to be who I want to be. Seeing Dad give that woman money to be quiet, when he should have cared what I thought, only showed me that his church will always come first. What I want doesn't matter at all to him."

Tracy turned to him and said, "That doesn't explain why you kept him in the dark about your plans. For that matter, you kept me in the dark too. They say that you bought a jazz club. So this plan of yours has been in the works for a while. I'm your woman. We live together, so how come I don't know anything about it?"

"I knew that you wouldn't have approved either. And you would have tried to talk me out of it. I wanted to wait until the deal was finalized and tell everyone when the time was right. But the situation with April's mom forced my hand."

Tracy stared out the window and had a dazed look in her face when she stated, "Everyone was wondering where you were today. That includes me. We were trying to keep that situation quiet because we knew it was a lie. But I heard some of the deacon's wives whispering behind my back right in the sanctuary. I have a weird feeling that it's going to come out anyway. You opening up a nightclub probably won't help how people perceive you."

Joshua abruptly stood up and yelled, "It's a supper club, not a night club. And I don't give a crap about my image. I didn't touch that girl and you know it. If the people who watched me grow up in the church believe this lie, then I'm truly glad that I am not going to be ministering to them anymore."

He lowered his voice and walked closer to her. "Look, I've been telling you from the start that the pulpit wasn't for me. I know you want to marry a man who is going to be the head of a mega church one day, but that man isn't me." He interrupted her when she tried to speak. "Please just listen," he pleaded. "My life is headed in a new direction. I am going to have to put in a lot of my energy into this new business of mine, which means, I won't be home a lot. I know that you aren't going to be happy about that."

"Well you already aren't home a lot. You're gone and I don't even know where you are half the time."

Joshua sighed. "I told you that it wasn't what you thought. I've been working at a restaurant learning the business so I would know what to do when I open the doors to my place. If I told you where I was going at night, I would have had to tell you my plans. And I wasn't ready to do that yet."

"I still don't understand why you couldn't just tell me that. What makes you think that I wouldn't want to be with you if you did something else for a living?" she asked as she tried to touch his arm but he stepped back.

"It's not just that. I also know that you want a baby and I don't. I've been trying to tell you that, but I don't think that you have been listening."

With a raised eyebrow she nervously asked, "Well what else have you been trying to tell me Josh?"

He didn't skip a beat when he simply replied, "That I want you to move out. We don't need to keep trying to make this thing work." Joshua let out a long breath. "Thank you for helping with my dad. But don't worry about him. I'll help him get back on his feet." And he quickly walked out of the kitchen.

"What? Wait a minute. Don't walk away like that." Tracy began to get louder and louder with every word she said. She demanded, "Come back here Josh!"

36

It was Wednesday morning before Zachariah fought his way out of Joshua's house. Neither Joshua or Tracy wanted him to leave to go back home or to work, but they were both driving him crazy worrying over him like he was an invalid. Plus there was so much tension in their household. Not only between Joshua and him, but between Joshua and Tracy as well. So he had to get out of there.

He appreciated the time to relax and he loved Tracy's home cooked meals. But he did not want to be in the middle of whatever was going on between them. Zachariah knew that they needed time to talk when he wasn't around. He wished that his son would have listened to him when he advised him not to let Tracy move in until they were officially married. He told him that it didn't look right for an assistant pastor to shack up. Looking back at it now, moving her in was probably just an act of defiance. One day, he would sit Joshua down and have a long talk with him too. Right now, the pain was too fresh and he still felt betrayed.

His sweet, future daughter-in-law had reluctantly warned him over breakfast that the news about Felicia and April's accusation had somehow gotten out. She revealed, "One of my so-called friends called me to ask if I thought that Joshua could actually be guilty of molesting April."

Zachariah raised his eyebrows and inquired, "What did you tell her?"

"I didn't tell her anything. I just slammed the phone down in her ear."

He rose to leave and said, "You are about to belong to a very strong family. We can handle this."

That's when Tracy started tearing up and confessed, "I don't think that I'm ever going to be a part of your family. Before you went to the hospital, Josh told me that he doesn't want to get married. And the other day he told me that he wants me to move out."

Hearing this made Zachariah sit back down. The two of them had eaten breakfast together every morning while Joshua stayed upstairs. He was shocked that this was the first time she mentioned this to him.

"He did what?" After a few moments of silence, he shook his head and said in an easy tone, "I don't know what's wrong with that boy. He is too young to be going through a midlife crisis." That brought a slight grin to Tracy's face.

Zachariah gave Tracy a big hug as he headed out the door and said, "Don't worry. I'm sure that my son will come to his senses and you two will work everything out." One of the church deacons had picked his car up from the church lot and parked it in the driveway. So he was able to drive himself across town to Mt. Zion today.

When Pastor arrived at his church, he stood on the front steps and took it all in. Grateful to be back, he knew he had some important things to tackle. David and one of his deacons were in his office handling church business for him when he arrived. They each jumped up, greeted him with a hug, and told him how happy they were that he was back at the church.

His son got up from the big leather chair behind his desk and moved to a smaller chair in front of it after he straightened the papers for his dad. Both men tried to bring him up to date on some unimportant matters, but he interrupted them. "You both know what I want to hear about."

The two men looked at him with puzzled expressions on their faces as they silently waited for his explanation. Their pastor asked, "Have a lot of the members already heard about the accusation against Joshua?"

The deacon let out a heavy sigh and answered, "I'm not sure about that, but I know that the other deacons and their wives know about it." He didn't skip a beat when he quickly added, "But no one believes it of course."

Zachariah smiled and declared, "Everyone in this room knows that isn't true. People even doubted Jesus. So I know they wouldn't hesitate to doubt a mere man." He rubbed his chin and inquired, "Did they mention the fact that April admitted that she lied?"

His deacon shook his head no and looked away.

Zachariah continued, "Well, why don't we put that important bit of information in the grapevine?"

The elderly deacon smiled and happily left on a mission with his instructions. He passed Mary in the hallway and excitedly announced, “He’s back.”

Mary entered Zachariah’s office smiling from ear to ear. “Hi. When I spoke to you yesterday, you didn’t tell me that you were coming back today. If I had known that, I wouldn’t have let these slobs clutter up your office,” she jokingly said as she tapped the minister of music on his back.

The three of them shared a laugh and then Pastor got back down to the business at hand. He asked, “How was choir rehearsal last night?”

Mary and David looked at each other for help. He spoke up first since it was in fact his choir. “You know that no one is going to say anything stupid to me. But there was a lot more whispering going on than usual.”

“I heard those cackling hens gossiping,” Mary spoke up. “Some say that you,” she pointed to Pastor, “fired Joshua because you thought he was guilty and that’s what caused your heart attack. While others don’t believe anything that they have heard. I think the church is divided. We were waiting until you came back so that you could set things straight.”

“Well how is April doing?”

Mary let out a heavy sigh. “You know she loves being in the choir and coming to rehearsal every week. But it’s been rough. Her new friends don’t sit next to her anymore and you can tell that they are whispering about her. She desperately wants to quit. And I might just let her.”

“No. Don’t let her quit, Mary. She has a beautiful strong voice. I’ve even had her practicing with some of the lead singers. I would really hate to lose her,” David replied.

Zachariah shook his head. He knew then that he would be spending the rest of his week coming up with a sermon related to what was going on in their lives. He looked at Mary and sternly said, “Do whatever you have to do, but have April in the choir stand on Sunday.”

Mary ran her right hand across her forehead and exhaled. She looked as if she wanted to ask for an explanation, but she didn’t. They both knew that her family had caused his family a lot of trouble lately but he wouldn’t do anything cruel to humiliate April. He wasn’t that kind of a man. When she dragged April to his hospital bed to apologize to him, he lectured her, but told her that he forgave her. He didn’t talk down to her or try to belittle her in any way. When April felt guilty and broke down in tears, he comforted her and told her what she did was very wrong but assured her that his heart attack was not her fault. He knew that Mary would have April in the choir stand that coming Sunday whether she liked it or not.

Zachariah continued his conversation with David and Mary. “I can’t keep staying with Joshua and Tracy. Things are very tense around there. This morning I found out that he told her that they weren’t getting married and he wants her to move out.”

Stunned, they both looked at each other letting Pastor know that it was a surprise to them as well. “Dad, I don’t know what is going on with him. He wasn’t in church last Sunday. I can’t remember him not being here with us before.”

Zachariah announced, “Well, Joshua needs to be here too. We’ve got to figure out how to get him to church Sunday the best way we can.”

37

"I ironed your white shirt and black pants for you, April."

April whipped her head around. Narrowing her eyes, she tried to figure out what her grandmother was talking about. "You ironed my choir uniform? I told you that I'm quitting the choir."

Her grandmother moved closer to her. April eased back. "No, Grandma."

"Listen baby," she started.

"I'm tired of people talking about me. Pointing and laughing at me or turning their heads so they don't have to look me in the eye. And I don't want to sit up there singing like everything is all good when it ain't."

Her grandmother pulled April to the kitchen table and made her sit down. She wouldn't let go of her hand even though April tried to shake it loose. "April, honey, I know things are hard for you right now. But you have to face your mistakes head on. We're not doing any more running in this family." Her grandmother was squeezing her hand so tight now that it hurt. "Your daddy ran away. Your mama is running now. But I'm not going to let you run too."

Tears were running down April's face as she sat shaking her head from side to side.

"I see the way your face lights up when you are in the choir stand. And I know that you love singing because you sing around here all the time."

"I do, but -"

"Some people have to wait a lifetime to get to do what makes them happy. You've been through a lot. But you've also been blessed to get to experience your little piece of happiness. So don't let anyone take that away from you, baby."

April's bottom lip quivered while she stared at her grandmother. She wanted to have the courage to confidently stand up in the choir stand and sing with everyone else. But she knew that people were going to be staring at her judging her. She made a big mistake and wanted to be forgiven and left alone. As she was sitting there thinking of a way to get out of facing everyone, her grandmother let go of her hand and stood up.

"You can't hide in this house, baby. We are all going to church together today." Mary looked down at April and announced, "As for me and my house, we will serve the Lord."

Choir members had to be there fifteen minutes before

service began in order to march in together. David was very strict. If you weren't there on time, you didn't get to sing. April tried dragging her feet to make her family late but it didn't work. Her grandmother broke the speed limit through the neighborhood. Ignoring the security guard, she double parked by the door and dragged April up the church stairs to get her there on time. April's brows came together and her mouth hung open. She had never seen her grandmother move like that before.

As the choir walked down the aisle, April kept her eyes straight ahead. She could hear whispering over to her right, but she refused to give in to the temptation to look their way. Once she was finally up in the stands, she took a deep breath and swayed to the beat of their first song.

At the back of the church, April could see her grandmother, brother, and sister entering and taking their seats. Pastor sat in the pulpit by himself. She wondered where Joshua was today, but then she looked down at the front row, there he was. It was weird seeing him in a pew with the rest of the congregation instead of by his father's side. He was wringing his hands together and had his head down. Joshua looked about as uncomfortable as she felt and she knew that it was all her fault.

After singing a few songs with the choir she had come to love, April was energized and glad that she came to church. Singing always made her forget her problems and feel better even if it was only temporary. They had one more song to sing before it was time to listen to the Pastor's sermon. April heard Brother David playing the first few notes of the classic gospel song Be Grateful. The problem was that she had only rehearsed it once with the choir. Her eyes grew wide. She whipped her head towards the minister of music. He was looking directly at her smiling. She immediately started shaking her head from side to side. Her eyes pleaded for him to stop playing that song. She wasn't ready yet. The girl next to her nudged her while he kept playing his keyboard. April looked out in the crowd at her grandmother for aid. But she was already up on her feet slowly swaying to the music. When she looked at Pastor for his help, he was nodding his head to the beat and waiting on her as well.

One minute had passed and the rest of the choir had already begun singing the chorus. April took a deep breath. She had exactly thirty more seconds to get to where she needed to be. After one last nudge from her neighbor she took three steps forward and slid the microphone off the base for her very first solo. She closed her eyes and quickly asked the Lord not to let her make a complete fool of herself.

Her first couple of words about what God hadn't promised her came out shaky. She was so nervous and could hear that she was a little off key. This is exactly what she didn't want to happen. April quickly remembered the minister of music advising her to seek out familiar faces in the crowd to make singing alone easier. So she found her family and focused on them. Instead of singing to the entire congregation, she sang her heart out to the people that she now knew truly loved her.

The beginning of the song started out very slow, but four minutes in the pace of the music and the singing picks up and gets louder. Soon, not only was her grandmother on her feet but nine or ten other people were too. Brother David and the drummer shared a short instrumental part of the song. By the time the entire choir joined in on their part, April heard a few shouts and a lot more people stood up. The drummer was feeling the spirit and was playing louder and faster. Some people remained seated but swayed their hands in the air or clapped their hands.

The minister of music moved his hand in a circular motion to let them know to continue singing. But April didn't think she could stop even if she wanted to. No longer was she standing in one spot staring at her family. She was moving all around the stage. Her soprano voice reached up into the balcony. Then she sang to the left side of the church. Not wanting the right side to be left out, she traveled to that side of the stage and insisted that they be grateful too. She felt like she belonged here. This is the kind of attention that she craved. No one was telling her that she was doing something wrong. Everyone was showing her that she was doing a great job for the first time in a long time.

When Brother David finally signaled that it was time to wrap up the song, April continued. The drummer and guitar player followed her queue and kept going too. By now a church member was filled with the Holy Spirit and started dancing at the front of the church. The minister of music gave in too and pounded a little harder on his keyboard. April was emotional, but still singing.

After a couple more minutes he signaled to the drummer and guitar player to slow down the pace of the music. Then he signaled to April to wrap it up again. This time she was complied. When she slid the microphone back on its stand and returned to her seat, the choir members to her left and right smiled at her and patted her on the back. April had done it. She had successfully sang her first solo at

Mt. Zion Baptist Church. By the looks of it, this wouldn't be her last.

38

Mary was so proud of April. She wanted to grab her and give her a big hug, but she would have to wait until church was over to do so. She watched her grandchild lift her hand up in the air and thank God. Mary was so grateful that April had made it through the storm and came out the other side a better person.

She watched Zachariah smile at April. Then he cleared his throat and stood up in his pulpit to face his congregation. He slowly scanned the pews until he found the faces that he was looking for. He smiled at Mary and then began. “Saints, I want to talk to you this beautiful Sunday morning about wakeup calls.”

He paused for a second and they heard a few, “Well” and “Preach Pastor” coming from his listeners.

"I know what some of you are thinking, because I can see it in your eyes. You are thinking, Pastor doesn't have any business up there getting himself all excited. For God sake, the man just had a heart attack." The church was so quiet you could hear a pin drop now. "So today I'm going to keep what I have to say short and sweet."

A big smile crossed Zachariah's face. He looked to the deacons all dressed in black suits on the front pew and asked, "When I mentioned wake up calls, did you think I meant when your alarm clock woke you up this morning?" But he didn't wait for their response. He quickly turned to the choir behind him and asked, "Did you think I meant an overnight stay at a hotel and you get the wakeup call at the time you requested?" Mary thought about Joshua's disappearance and where he confessed to be hiding out. She couldn't help but look over at him as he shifted uncomfortably in his seat.

Zachariah turned back to his curious congregation and shouted, "No, I'm talking about the kind of wakeup call that knocks you to your knees." Some of his members were shaking their heads up and down in agreement and hanging on to his every word. He promptly and nonchalantly waved his right hand and added his famous, "Y'all don't hear me though."

One of the deacons stood up in anticipation. From their experience, Pastor always gave an incredible sermon when he said, "Y'all don't hear me though."

They heard a few "Amens" and even an "Alright now" from the pews.

Everyone could hear the excitement in his voice when he bellowed, "I said I'm talking about the kind of wakeup call that you've got to look up to the heavens and cry out 'God what are you trying to do to me?'" Even Mary had to shake her head and close her eyes like he was talking specifically about her. "There were many wake up calls in the Bible. If I read them all to you, you'd be afraid. So how about the book of Exodus when Moses asked Pharaoh to free his slaves? God had to send down ten plagues to get Pharaoh to do the right thing. I think after just one plague or wake up call, I would have listened. What about you?"

Mary looked at Brooklyn shaking her head up and down agreeing with Pastor and smiled. She noticed that the minister of music began to softly play the keyboard when his father paused.

"Okay, well how about Jonah? God told him to go into the city and prophesize for him. Jonah chose to run away from God and got on a boat instead. God sent his wake-up call in the form of a storm. Jonah was literally asleep when the storm came. The men on the boat sacrificed him and threw him overboard to calm the waters. Next thing you know he is being swallowed up by a whale. Now, how is that for a wakeup call?"

A few more members of the congregation shouted and jumped from their seats.

Zachariah continued, "You never know when God is going to give you a wakeup call. And my wakeup call is going to be different from your wakeup call. We've all got different personalities and different experiences; therefore we are all going to respond differently to our own individual wakeup calls. In fact, I might see the way that you are responding to your call and think Sister So and So sure is acting strange lately."

One of the church nurses standing close by wiped the sweat off the pastor's forehead. He kept shouting anyway, "Sister So and So sees the way that I'm coping with my wakeup call and thinks Pastor has lost his mind." Most of the people in the church were shaking their heads up and down and some were now smiling.

Then Pastor stepped down from the pulpit. He stood near Joshua who was sitting on the front pew and not in the pulpit for the first time in years. Zachariah never looked directly at him though. He whispered into his microphone, "But who am I to judge you?"

Mary could see Joshua fighting the smile that came to his face and try to be cool. She was so happy that he agreed to come to church today to hear his father say those words.

Zachariah paused and demanded, "Turn to your neighbor and ask, 'who am I to judge you?" He walked away from Joshua and walked back up on stage close to April in the choir stand. But never looked directly at her either and again told his congregation, "Turn to your other neighbor, the one who was trying to avoid making eye contact with you, and ask 'who are you to judge me?'"

Even from her seat, Mary could see tears coming to April's eyes. She hoped that April understood what he was trying to say.

They heard a few shouts, but it didn't seem likc enough to please Zachariah. He walked back to the pulpit. "Oh it's quiet in here now. I must have hit a little too close to home. I can't get very many amens anymore."

The congregation began to laugh a little and a few shouted, "Amen" and one "Tell it, Pastor."

He took a sip of his water to quench his thirst and

continued at a normal tone. “Saints, what I am trying to say is God has His own mysterious way of telling you that you are doing something wrong and that you are not listening to Him. Some of us are so busy meddling and looking in other folk’s houses that we can’t see that our own straw house is about to be blown down.”

Mary had to shout amen to that.

“Don’t worry about what your family is going to say. Don’t worry about what your haters will say.” He paused and said, “Yes, that’s right. Your pastor knows what haters are. I have a few myself.” Mary looked around and saw that that got a few smiles from the young people in the congregation.

Zachariah got serious again and pounded on the wooden podium with his right fist. He hollered, “Children of God, when the Father in heaven sends you a wakeup call, you’d better listen. Heed my warning. Whether it is in the form of a child behaving badly, a job that you got let go from, a spouse that leaves you, a car accident that nearly kills you, a heart attack, or a tornado that tears your house down while your other neighbors houses go untouched,” he was speaking so fast that he had to catch his breath which made Mary scared. “It’s a wakeup call and you’d better stop and figure out what God is trying to tell you.”

The keyboard was playing loud and his congregation was up on their feet shouting with just as much excitement and enthusiasm as Zachariah. He slowed down and looked around. Then he continued, “Now you might ask, ‘Pastor, do all wakeup calls have to be bad?’ My answer to you is a resounding, no. All wakeup calls do not have to be bad. Now, I know you have all heard the sayings, under every dark cloud is a silver lining. How about, one man’s trash is another man's treasure?" Pastor threw up his arms and said, "It's all about how you look at it. A wakeup call is God's little way of saying, 'a change has got to happen." Mary was happy that he paused and took a deep breath. "Ephesians 5:14 says, "Awake, you who sleep, Arise from the dead, and Christ will give you light." Mt. Zion's minister shook his pointed finger at his congregation and warned, "I'm telling you that you'd better listen." He smiled and admitted, "I know I am."

Epilogue

August 1991

Zachariah's medium size church office was full of men and boys in various stages of getting dressed. He stood in the mirror struggling to tie his bow tie. Joshua knew that it wasn't second thoughts about what he was about to do. So he chalked it up to old age. Today was his father's wedding day and he wasn't going to let a little thing like a stupid bow tie frustrate him. He quickly walked up behind him and assisted with his situation. It was funny that his dad was the one who had taught him how to knot ties. And now Joshua was helping him.

Shortly after the shock of Joshua's big announcement wore off, Zachariah treated both of his sons to a weekend retreat. The three men traveled to tiny Sapelo Island for some male bonding time and relaxation. They loved it because they were virtually cut off from the rest of the world.

Zachariah ended up doing something that Joshua never pictured him doing. He apologized to his offspring for forcing them to devote their lives to Mt. Zion. His dad admitted that it hit him like a ton of bricks how demanding and overbearing he had been with them all their life. He was happy that David had embraced his vision of the church being a family business because it involved him playing music, which was his passion. But he understood why Joshua rebelled against it. And even gave him his blessing to follow his own dream.

Joshua came back home and buckled down to run his supper club. Even though he was the sole owner and it was taking all of his time and energy to build his business, people didn't come to see him. He didn't have the pressure of being in the spotlight. In fact, most of his customers didn't know or care who the owner was. The customers came to groove to live music, listen to spoken word artists, and enjoy the delicious food. Although he knew that he still had a lot to learn about running a successful business like his father, Joshua was excited about the rewards and the challenges to come.

For the first time in his life, he was proud of himself for doing what he wanted to do. And he was accepting the consequences of his past mistakes. He should have never given into his mom and proposed to Tracy. Although Tracy was a sweet woman most of the time, she was now a woman scorned. Once she realized that Joshua was adamant about not getting married so he could start his life over with a clean slate, she became enraged. When a church member asked her why April and she came running out of the church crying at the same time, Tracy was the one who poured gas on the flames at church by spreading lies that April was the real reason they weren't getting married.

She waited until he wasn't home to pick up her belongings and trashed the place. He came home and the kitchen where Tracy had cooked many delicious meals for him to find the refrigerator and freezer doors were left wide open all day. At first he tried to see what he could salvage but decided to go ahead and throw all of the food away. Joshua could smell the bleach as he walked up the stairs to his bedroom. Bleach splatters now decorated his king size comforter. The master bathroom where they steamed up the room making love, now had a broken glass shower door. Joshua quickly circled back to his walk-in closet afraid of what he might find. At first glance it appeared that Tracy had spared this room. But a closer look proved otherwise. The last present Tracy bought him was a brand-new pair of black Stacy Adam dress shoes. The carpet all around the shoes was wet. Both shoes were soaked with what smelled like urine. If there had been any doubt in Joshua's mind who ransacked his home, Tracy definitely wanted it to be understood that it was her.

Joshua decided not to press charges against her and hoped that he wouldn't have to see her anymore. He suspected that she was the one who reported him to the Department of Family and Children's Services, but later found out that it was a teacher at April's school. A case worker came around and interviewed everyone in both families before dropping the case. He wasn't in the pulpit anymore, but he came to church every Sunday and sat on the front row to support his family. Tracy came to church every Sunday too. Whenever they saw each other, she rolled her eyes and looked away.

But he wasn't going to think about his problems today though. Today was a special day for his father and he wanted to be in the right frame of mind for him. Although, he never intended to step up to the microphone at Mt. Zion Baptist Church again, his father had asked him to serve as the officiant for Mary and him. Joshua was reluctant to accept at first. But as time passed, he felt honored that his father had asked him to perform his last act of ministry by marrying two very special people in his life.

Now that Joshua had tied his father's bow tie for him, he looked around the room. Anthony Jr. sat with his bow tie untied looking bored without his video game. Joshua spoke to him and bent down to tie his tie too. Anthony nodded a thank you. The rest of the guys looked almost ready, so he decided to go check on the ladies.

When he gently knocked on the door of the conference room that was now Mary's temporary bridal suite, Brooklyn cracked the door to see who it was. Then she smiled and opened the door so that he could enter. Joshua walked in the room and looked at the ladies crammed in the room getting ready. "Hello. All of you look very pretty today." He took a minute to admire how nice they all looked in their matching purple bridesmaid dresses.

April was primping in the mirror along with the other women in the wedding party when Joshua entered the room. It was weird that in a few short minutes he would become her uncle. She confessed that she was afraid that he would never speak to her again after what she had accused him of, but he had. He even accepted her heartfelt apology. Deep down, he knew that if it wasn't for the scandal, he probably would have gotten cold feet and continued to put off chasing his dreams. He would have wound up being stuck as the pastor of his father's church for the rest of his life with Tracy by his side. He could thank April for helping end his relationship with Tracy too. His dad always preached that what others meant for evil, God meant it for good. April had been a blessing in disguise and for that reason he could never hate her. Everyone, especially him, was just glad that the whole nightmare was over.

Nobody had seen Felicia since she walked out of Mt. Zion with the check his dad wrote her nine months ago. Word on the street was that she went back to smoking crack. Others said that she left town in search of Tony. They all figured she would show her face again one day. Until then, her kids would be well taken care of.

Between Mary and help from his dad, April was turning into a well-mannered young lady. She was finally getting a dependable mother and a wonderful father figure in her life. It was obvious to everyone that she loved singing in the choir on Sundays. She was sporting a brand-new cute haircut and wearing contact lenses that helped her see better in school. The tutor that his dad hired helped too. And she was no longer trying to live up to her reputation of being a tough girl. Although she swore that she stopped having sex, Mary made her get on birth control and gave her a box of condoms telling her that she was too young to be a great-grandmother. She told April to put the box away until she felt like she needed them.

His dad told him that as she hated going at first, but

April actually liked seeing her psychiatrist on a regular basis now. She said it was nice being able to talk to someone who would really listen to her and give advice instead of telling her what to do. The best part was that she kept everything they discussed confidential. April didn't have to worry about the woman smiling in her face and stabbing her in the back like her friends had done.

He stopped staring at April and walked over to Mary. She was getting the finishing touches of her makeup done. He sincerely said, "You look beautiful. Are you almost ready to get started?"

Joshua could tell by the stressed-out look on her face that Mary wasn't used to all of these people fussing over her. She looked up at him, smiled and playfully answered, "If the hairstylist and makeup artist would stop putting all this stuff on me, I would be ready."

Her glam squad got the hint and hurried to get to a stopping point. When they finally finished and walked away, Mary confessed, "I am so excited about marrying your daddy today that I don't know what to do. I thought that I was too old to find love again and was going to be content remembering the good old days with my husband before he died. Now, I'm looking forward to making new memories with my soon to be husband."

Joshua smiled, "Aside from my mother of course, you are one of the best things to happen to my dad's life. So I'm glad you two are together. He's happy."

Mary grabbed his hand and smiled. "And I'm as happy as a tick on a fat dog."

Everyone in the room stopped what they were doing and stared at Mary. April was the first one to burst out laughing. She hollered, "Grandma, you are so country. Where do you come up with those?"

Mary had to chuckle herself. "Well I don't make this stuff up. Y'all never heard that before?"

Even Joshua shook his head and joined in. When everyone finally finished cackling at Mary's expense, he continued their conversation. "It's going to be weird driving to a new house to see my dad."

"I know, but we agreed that we needed a fresh start in our own home. So we put both our houses that we shared with our spouses and kids up for sale and bought a new home of our own. The kids get a fresh start in new schools and all of them get their own bedrooms."

"Woohoo," April yelled from across the room and everyone started laughing again. "And I get to hang posters up on my walls."

Mary chimed back in, "And we have a huge kitchen for us to cook together in."

April smiled and winked at her grandmother.

"I can't wait to see it," Joshua said. "But I already saw your wedding present parked in the parking lot."

Mary covered her face to hide her blushing. "Can you believe it? I've always wanted a Jaguar. Your father is spoiling me rotten."

"What did you do with your old car?" he curiously asked.

"Oh I still have it." Mary looked around and motioned with her finger for him to come closer. She whispered, "April started doing really good in school towards the end of last school year. So I plan on giving it to her when school starts."

Joshua glanced over his shoulder to make sure April didn't overhear their secret. Then he continued, "And speaking of fresh starts, when I was out there admiring your car, I also saw the new billboard." Mary's bit her bottom lip. "That was your dad's idea. Do you like it? He said that you wouldn't mind him taking down the old one."

"Oh no don't worry about me. I never wanted to be up there on that sign in the first place. But you and Dad look great together up there. I saw some people standing in the parking lot admiring it before they came inside."

"I hope they only have nice things to say about it. You know how people can be around here. Your daddy warned me that being a first lady isn't for the faint of heart. But I think that I am up for the challenge. I love the Lord, your dad, and Mt. Zion."

"Me too, Mary. Me too."

As Joshua stood looking out at the sea of wedding guests on their feet clapping their hands and shouting while his father kissed his new bride, he thought he saw a glimpse of Felicia leaving from the back pew. He wrapped up the rest of the ceremony as quickly as he could. Then he followed the wedding party down the aisle. He separated himself from the crowd and ran down the church stairs and out the door. Looking left and then right, he tried to spot Felicia again. He wondered if his mind was playing tricks on him or if he really did see her.

He swung around when he felt someone tapping on his shoulder. "Why'd you run off? Are you okay?"

Joshua smiled at the sight of April worrying about him. "Yes, I'm alright. I need to get some air. Are you okay?"

He watched a huge smile spread across April's face. "I'm fine. Grandma is happy. And I'm happy for her. Guess what?"

"What?"

"Your Dad said that I can call him Grandpa now if I want to."

Joshua nodded his head up and down and kept smiling. He put his hands in his pockets and looked out into the street.

"I think it will be cool having a man around the house again. You know?" She looked at him but didn't wait for an answer. "I'm excited about going to high school and making new friends too."

"Yeah, I think that's going to be good for you."

"Our new house is so big that I get my own room. Grandpa says he will have a painter make it whatever color I want. And my room has its own bathroom so I can stay in there singing forever and not have to get out for anybody."

Joshua chuckled at that. "That's great."

"Singing in the choir is the best thing that's ever happened to me. Thank you for coming up with that idea."

He turned about towards her. "You're welcome."

She stopped smiling and shrugged. "Brooklyn and Anthony Jr. still get on my nerves, but I can't have everything I guess."

Joshua shook his head and laughed. "No, I guess you can't have everything." He stood there smiling for a few more seconds. Maybe all of this has changed April. She wasn't the same kid with a bad attitude that was mad at the world who came into his office last year. From what he heard and saw with his own eyes, April talked respectfully to her elders now, listened to them, and was grateful to have her grandmother back in her life.

April turned and started climbing the stairs. She yelled over her shoulder, “The limo is waiting on us on the other side of the building. Are you coming, Uncle Josh?”

Joshua glanced up and down the street once more. With no sign of Felicia in sight, he turned and followed April back inside.

ABOUT THE AUTHOR

Nicole Scott was born in Cleveland, Ohio. She is an avid reader and the member of a book club for over twenty-five years. Discovering that writing could help heal a broken heart she was inspired to write herself. Her writing credits include interviewing celebrities for national magazines. She is the mother of two and lives in Atlanta, Georgia where she is working on her next novel. Nicole loves writing, fashion, movies, walking, reading, parties, and eating chocolate. Keep up with Nicole on Instagram @thenicolescott and sign up for updates at www.authornicolescott.com

www.ingramcontent.com/pod-product-compliance
Lightning Source LLC
LaVergne TN
LVHW050614100826
845148LV00011B/1583

* 9 7 8 1 7 3 6 3 0 3 2 8 3 *